Mending

Mending was almost impossible until I met

Edward Scott

Book 3 of the Abigail's Fate series.

By Adele Lea.

Dedicated to my friend Tracy, in memory of her beautiful daughter Claire Roberts.

"Her light may have faded on this earth,

but it shines brightly upon us for all eternity."

Chapter 1

We've arrived at the police station and are parked outside. It's not the one near my home and I wonder why he's come here, but I don't ask.

"Are you ready, Abbie?" he asks, concerned.

"Yes. Let's get this over with." I answer taking his hand as we walk up the steps to the entrance.

It's a large building, glass and iron – new modern, I think they call it. We reach the top of the steps and walk towards two large glass doors that open automatically. I squeeze Edward's hand gently as I begin to feel a little nervous.

"Are you okay? Are you sure you want to do this?"

I nod as we walk through the doors. I feel as though I'm entering unfamiliar territory. I've never been in a police station before and it's quite intimidating. A large glass reception area faces us and two uniformed police officers stand behind the desk.

I stop in my tracks and pull on Edward's hand as I look around the space. It's bright, light and empty – uninviting. There are posters on the walls announcing crime figures, gun trafficking, people trafficking and zero tolerance, and I suddenly feel out of my depth. I don't know if I can go through with this or even walk up to the desk.

One of the police officers sees us standing in the middle of the room. His voice is loud and echoes in the empty space.

"Can I help you, sir, madam?"

I don't answer at first.

"Abbie." Edward says, nudging me to answer. I nod and move forward.

"Yes? How can I help?" the same officer asks. His tone is patronising, even hostile. I just stare at him. I hadn't expected that he's making me feel as though it's me who's done something wrong. Edward squeezes my hand, prompting me to speak.

"Hum ... I want to make a complaint."

The officer continues to stare, then says, "Complaint?"

I turn and look at Edward, thinking, *Am I saying it all wrong?* But answer quietly,

"Yes," although I feel intimidated, by him.

"Really, madam?"

Edward's expression changes suddenly. He glares at the officer, who remains stern, as if it's common practice for him to speak to people like that. I'm stuck for words and not sure how to respond, and I wonder whether I should go ahead. I frown at Edward, then pull on his hand like a scared and vulnerable child. Edward turns his eyes to me.

"Can we just go, please?"

Edward quickly turns his attention to the officer. He doesn't take his eyes off him, but releases my hand as he speaks to me gently.

"I'll sort this, sweetheart. You go and sit over there." Then he smiles and points to a row of chairs.

I just do as he says and sit down, looking towards him. Edward's now leaning over the desk towards the officer. His voice is low but firm. I can't hear what he's saying, although the expression on his face is one of annoyance. The officer's face has dropped; he nods at Edward, and I think he's apologising. Edward scowls before turning and walking back towards me. He sits beside me and takes my hand.

"Someone will be out shortly."

"I hope it's not him."

"I can assure you, it won't be." His voice is firm but guarded.

"What did you say to him?"

He doesn't answer but simply pats my hand, and I can imagine the words that passed between them, knowing Edward as I do, and given the look on the officer's face I think I'm right. He's probably just brought him down a peg or two, and quite right too.

We sit in silence, waiting for someone to come to use.

A policewoman walks into the office. She picks up a clipboard, then comes through a door to our side and approaches us.

"Sir, madam, if you'd like to follow me, please. I'll take you through to one of the interview rooms."

We stand. My hands begin to shake as we follow the officer through a key-coded door and along a long corridor with doors on either side. My breathing increases in speed as realisation is setting in at what I'm about to do and say. I'm sure Edward is picking up on my vibes.

The officer turns around as Edward says, "Please, can you just give us five minutes?"

She nods and opens a door that reads "Interview Room 4". She enters, leaving us standing outside.

"Do you want me to come in with you, Abbie?"

"Please. Yes. I need you to. I don't think I can do this – not without you. But I need you to promise me something first."

"What?"

"Whatever's said in there, please promise me you'll never tell my gran."

He looks puzzled.

"Promise me, Edward, please."

He nods. "I promise, Abbie. Whatever's said stays within those four walls."

"Thank you."

"Are you ready?"

I want to say no, I'm not ready. I don't think I'll ever be ready to do this, but I'm going to do it nevertheless. So I nod and we enter the interview room.

We're greeted by the officer. She guides us with her hand, pointing towards a table. We sit next to each other facing her. The clipboard is on the desk. She offers me a reassuring smile.

"My name is Officer Johnson. I'll attend along with Detective Ambrose. He'll be conducting the interview and will be in momentarily."

I look at Edward. He smiles. Then I return my gaze to her as she continues to speak.

"May I take some details from you, please?"

I nod.

"Your full name?"

"Abigail Elizabeth Baxter."

"Is that Mrs?" I shake my head. "Sorry, Miss then." I nod. "And your full name, sir, for the record."

Edward's tone is authoritative but not hostile. "Edward Albert Scott."

She writes it down next to my name.

"And, Miss Baxter, the nature of your complaint?"

I look a little confused; I don't know how to say it. I glance at Edward; he nods for me to continue.

"Abuse."

She raises her eyes.

"From whom?"

My hands begin to fidget.

"Abigail … May I call you Abigail?"

I nod.

"Please don't be nervous. I guess it took a lot of courage for you to come here."

Again, I nod.

"Okay, Abigail, who's abused you?"

"My husband."

She stares at Edward.

"Not Edward," I reply, shocked. Does she think Edward's my husband? She smiles, and I realise she doesn't. I raise my eyes at myself knowing, I'm not thinking rationally at the moment.

"May I take your husband's name, Abigail?"

I breathe out, feeling sick. "Adam Lord." My voice sounds flat as I say the words.

"Is Baxter your maiden name, then?"

"Yes."

"I need to ask you, was it physical or mental abuse?"

"Both," I say, trying to blank the image of Adam from my mind.

"Abigail, I also need to ask you whether you'd like Mr Scott present with you in the interview."

"Yes," I answer strongly, and stare in Edward's direction.

"That's fine, Abigail. Can I get you a glass of water?"

I shake my head.

"I need to explain what will happen throughout the interview. It will be recorded and you'll need to answer all the questions openly and honestly. If a prosecution is sought these tapes will be used in evidence. If at any time you feel like you need a break, please say so and we'll stop the recording and the interview."

She stands.

"I'll just go and find out where Detective Ambrose is."

"That's fine, Officer Johnson," Edward says. She leaves the room, leaving us alone.

"Are you okay, Abbie?"

"I think so. I just wish it was over with."

"It will be soon, and then we can put it behind us."

I'm hoping he's right.

Officer Johnson and, I presume, Detective Ambrose enter the room. He's around six foot, quite portly, and his face is worn, probably from lack of sleep. He's dressed in a tired suit, in contrast to Officer Johnson's uniform. She adjusts her skirt before sitting down. I'd not noticed before but she also looks weary; it must be the job – the things they hear and see must keep them from sleep at night.

They sit opposite us. Ambrose speaks first.

"Miss Baxter, I'm Detective Ambrose. Officer Johnson has informed me of the nature of your complaint against Adam Lord and that you would like Mr Scott to be present throughout the interview. Is that correct?"

"Yes."

"Okay, I'm going to switch the recorder on and I'd like everyone to give their names when asked. I'll ask you questions, Miss Baxter, and I'd like you to answer them openly and honestly."

I squeeze Edward's hand, thinking how formal it all is.

"Right, may we please start?"

Edward squeezes my hand back reassuringly while I briefly close my eyes and nod.

Ambrose flicks a switch. He states the time and date and asks us to speak into the recorder when directed.

"Present in the room is Detective Ambrose."

Officer Johnson then says her name.

Ambrose continues, "Plaintiff. Miss Abigail Elizabeth Baxter. Miss Baxter, please say your full name for the record."

"Abigail Elizabeth Baxter."

"Thank you. Also present, Edward Albert Scott …" He raises an inquisitive eye at Edward, but doesn't speak to him, nor does Edward respond, then continues with a puzzled expression on his face. "… accompanying Miss Baxter. Miss Baxter, do you consent to Mr Scott attending?"

I nod.

"Miss Baxter, you need to speak for the record."

"Sorry. I do, yes."

"And now you, sir, please say your full name for the record."

"Edward Albert Scott."

Ambrose returns his eyes to me.

"Miss Baxter, can you tell me why you've come to the police station today?"

I'm silent.

"Miss Baxter, I need you to answer the questions, please, as we're recording the interview."

I feel so flustered. I stare at him, trying to get the words out of my mouth. I look at Johnson, who just stares back at me. I turn to Edward; his eyes are on me too. I want someone to speak for me, but they can't say what's happened. And that's why I'm here – it happened to me, and I have to tell the story. I can't put my head in the sand as I've done previously. I turn back to Ambrose, who's waiting for me to begin. I squeeze Edward's hand so hard that I'm sure it must hurt him.

I breathe in, then out.

"I'm sorry, this is harder than I thought. I've come to make a complaint against my husband, Adam Lord."

"The nature of that complaint is?"

"Physical and mental abuse."

"And how long has this been happening, Miss Baxter?"

"Four years."

"Can you tell me in your own words, Miss Baxter, what Mr Lord has done? And when it started."

I close my eyes. I don't think I can do this. I feel as if I'm on the spot with everyone waiting for me to speak.

"Miss Baxter, if you're struggling, let me put it a different way. What's made you come today?"

This is it. I have to speak.

"He attacked me."

"Attacked you, Miss Baxter?"

I nod then remember. "Sorry ... yes."

"So, can you tell me when the attack happened?"

"Saturday night," I answer. My voice sounds wobbly.

"Saturday just gone?" His eyebrows raise. "That would be the sixth of December?"

I'm not sure why his tone has changed. It's as if he's trying to catch me out.

"Yes," I reply firmly.

"And where did the attack take place?"

"At my home."

"Is that the home you share with Adam Lord?"

His tone is probing, and I'm not sure how to reply to that question.

"Yes. Well ... I mean ... no, not anymore."

"Did Mr Lord move out?"

"No. I changed the locks so that he couldn't get in, but …"
I feel so flustered. "But … but … it's my house."

Ambrose sits straighter in his chair, then quizzically asks,
"Are you not married to Mr Lord?"

I stare at him, knowing exactly where these questions are
leading.

He continues. "Is the house in both your names? And, if so,
did you change the locks on the doors of the property that you
both own?"

I don't know what to say, because it's true, it does belong
to us both in the eyes of the law, but in my eyes it doesn't – that
house belongs to me. Always has and always will. I frown,
disgruntled by his tone of voice because he doesn't know
Adam like I do.

"Yes, to both your questions," I snap.

"So … when he attacked you, at your house, what
happened?"

I roll my eyes at him and he waits for me to start.

"He forced himself into the house and knocked me to the
floor. He punched me, threatened me and threatened to hurt
Edward if I didn't leave him."

I look at Edward, then return my eyes to Ambrose.

Who replies with a voice that says he doesn't care.

"And why would he threaten Edward?"

His manner is probing, and I know he doesn't believe what I'm saying. It looks bad, I know that, but I feel as if he's twisting my words. I start to feel irritated.

"Don't you believe me, Detective Ambrose?" And I stare at him.

He gestures with his hand as though I'm reporting some menial crime, as if someone has played knock and run on my front door.

"Please continue, Miss Baxter."

And I suddenly feel intimidated, like it's me who's in the wrong. Why have I come here? I put my head in my hands, feeling confused and flustered. I'm clammy but shivery. I turn to Edward. His expression is one of astonishment, as if he can't believe how Ambrose is behaving.

"Please, Edward, I shouldn't have come here. I think I want to leave."

He raises an eyebrow.

"They don't believe me. I knew they wouldn't. Adam's been far too clever, covered his tracks far too well for anyone to believe what he's done to me."

"Do you want to leave, Abbie? Do you want me to take you home?" he asks understandingly.

I shrug. I know I have to do this but I'm struggling. I feel like I'm being backed into a corner. I know I shouldn't have changed the locks. I knew there would be consequences. I've played straight into Adam's hands, but what choice did I have? They don't know him like I do.

Then her words come floating into my head. *Be strong, and do what you have to do.*

There's a dry cough in the room to get my attention. Ambrose speaks clearly and firmly. "Miss Baxter, do you want me to stop the tape?"

I know I have to sort this or it'll never end. I reply in the same courteous tone he's just used towards me. "No." I push my chair out and stand.

I'm breathing quite fast, almost panting. I remove my jacket to cool myself down.

"Miss Baxter, would you like a glass of water?" Johnson asks calmly.

"Please."

She passes me the glass, seeing my hand shaking as I take a sip, it makes me cough as I'm swallowing. I feel fidgety, stressed, and lightheaded as I place the glass on the table before reaching for the back of the chair to steady myself. Edward instinctively moves towards me. I smile at him, knowing he must be going through hell, listening to all this and not being able to stick up for me.

"I'm fine Edward."

"Miss Baxter, do you feel all right?" Johnson asks.

"I'm okay."

I turn my eyes to Ambrose, and speak loudly and clearly. "Detective Ambrose, you have to believe me. He's a monster. He can't continue doing these things to me. He tracked me using my phone."

His eyes raise. "Have you got your phone?"

"No, I smashed it." I shake my head, annoyed with myself. It had held all the messages, the phone calls, and the threats, and now I've no proof.

"Miss Baxter, we can't do anything without your phone. We can't prove he tracked you with it if you haven't got it."

My head's pounding. I run my hand over my forehead and I feel like screaming at the top of my lungs. I glance towards Edward; his face is sad. My eyes close as I wonder, why I came, because I know Adam's won again.

Edward stands. I shake my head in defeat and he sits back in his chair, looking torn.

"He's terrorised her!" Edward snaps. "Can't you see what he's done to her, for God's sake?"

"Mr Scott, please, we can't do anything without proof. The evidence is all circumstantial, and it would be Miss Baxter's word against his."

I hold my hand to my mouth, realising it's true, but I'm angry now because Edward looks so frustrated, because he really wants to help me. I need them to understand what

Adam's done. I shout as I pull my jumper over my head, then my T-shirt, exposing my bruised arms, neck and back.

"Is this enough proof? Is this what you need?" I shout.

I hold my hand to my mouth. Tears of anger and frustration fall. Everyone stops and stares at my body – what Adam's done to me. I begin to pace the room. I feel scared but mad, too.

"Miss Baxter, please calm down," Johnson says, moving forward towards me.

My hand flies out to stop her. "No, I will not calm down. This is what happens when you're calm, when you don't fight back. Bad things happen. People ignore you, tell you it's your fault." I breathe in deeply. "Well, is this my fault? Is it? Answer me."

No one answers; they just stare.

"Is it?" I shout.

My head's spinning and I can't stop what's coming out of my mouth. Edward looks aghast. I really don't want him to hear this, but I have to stop Adam.

"You have to listen to me. You have to stop him. He's a monster and you can't allow him to hurt Nicky's baby. You can't – he can't do that again and get away with it."

Ambrose sits bolt upright in his chair and I'm not sure why, maybe it's my tone of voice or the words I've just shouted but it's certainly got his attention.

"Miss Baxter, what do you mean, hurt another baby?"

I turn my eyes to Edward.

"Abbie, what do you mean?" Edward asks. His expression has changed.

I screw my eyes tight shut and shake my head, trying to get rid of the images that are appearing in my mind as I rattle out the words.

"No, no. I cannot relive that night, not again."

"Abbie, what happened?"

I open my eyes and look at him.

"Don't, Edward. Please, please don't make me say it," I beg, holding my hand over my heart, remembering that night so vividly. "I can't. It hurts too much."

"Miss Baxter, did Mr Lord hurt your baby?" Ambrose asks. His tone is softer, more inquisitive.

I just stare. I can't answer.

Edward speaks lowly in response for me. "She lost two babies, miscarried them both."

Then he shakes his head, realising I think what really happened. His voice is full of hurt and sorrow as he whispers, "Abbie."

"Stop, please. I can't do this. It hurts too much—"

"Miss Baxter, I know this is hard, but you need to tell us," says Ambrose.

My eyes flare towards him. He's not lived these nightmares day after day, night after night. I'm furious and scream, "How on earth can you know what I'm feeling or how hard this is for me? You have no idea."

I start to sob. Edward's gets up to come to me but I walk backwards, away from him. I don't mean to but I feel weak, and I'm so angry, remembering what Adam has done to me and my unborn children.

Edward looks shocked, and Ambrose says his next words with caution.

"What do you want to do then, Miss Baxter, about Mr Lord?"

Again, I raise my hands to stop him talking, and he goes silent. My anger has got the better of me; all I can see is red, and Adam's face … laughing at me. I scream, venting all my frustration, knowing for the first time exactly what I want to do. My reply is harsh and firm.

"I'll tell you what I want to do about Adam. I want to drag him screaming up the stairs, throw him hard on the bed. Laugh in his face while I punch him in the stomach. I want him to beg me to stop, but I won't. I'll continue to hit him, again and again."

I look up from my rant and realise what I've said out loud. Edward is staring at me. Johnson has her hand to her mouth. I fall to my knees, sobbing, and I can't stop. I'm reliving that night; it won't stop playing in my head.

"I'm bleeding and there's so much blood. I can feel my baby's life leaving me, and I want to leave with it, but he just shouts at me. I can't stop it from happening. I'm it's mummy and I'm whispering that I'm so sorry that I can't protect it. I'm helpless. I can't stop it from happening again. I can't do anything and I want to die. I just want close my eyes and fade away. But he won't let me. He screams at me, telling me it's *my fault.* My fault that he did that to me. I lost the most precious thing in the world that night, another baby, and you sit there telling me you know that this is hard, that you have no proof he's a monster. Only a monster could do what he's done."

Edward jumps from his chair and pulls me from the floor and into his arms. He holds me to him tightly. And I feel sick and dizzy. I'm hot and struggling to breathe, and I know it's because of what I've just said, what I've confessed. I feel ashamed of myself. Ashamed that Edward heard it. But he's just whispering to me.

"Sweetheart."

He stares at me strangely, and I feel unwell.

"Abbie, my God, you're burning up."

He takes my face into his hands. The lights darken, and his face fades as my eyes close.

"Abbie, open your eyes. Are you all right?"

I shake my head. My legs buckle beneath me.

"I don't feel very …"

Then there's silence.

Chapter 2

"Abbie, sweetheart, talk to me. What's wrong?" Edward says quietly as he's lowering me gently to the floor.

My eyes start to flicker opening at the sound of his voice. I feel as though my skin is scorching, but I'm shivering with cold. There's a pain in my side when I breathe in.

Ambrose is shouting at Johnson, "Go and get a first-aider."

I don't know what's going on. I'm scared, and Edward's face is full of worry. He pulls his phone from his pocket and punches in a number. I notice his hand shaking.

"Emergency, blue light!"

I hear the tension in his voice, and it frightens me.

"We can deal with this, Mr Scott," Ambrose says loudly.

Edward puts his hand up. "Silence!" he bellows, and Ambrose instantly stops talking.

Edward continues on the phone; I think he's answering questions.

"I'm a doctor."

There's a pause.

"Manchester Lane, police station. Collapse. Possible pneumonia."

My head is pounding and the pain in my side is becoming unbearable. I feel as though I'm gasping for breath.

There's another pause from Edward; his eyes haven't moved from mine.

"Y-Yes, in and out of consciousness."

My eyes flicker again, then close.

"Abbie, Stay with me. Open your eyes. Johnson, take my phone."

She runs over and starts speaking to the person on the other end of the line.

"Abbie, come on. Stay awake. Talk to me."

Everything is hazy, the voices muffled. My senses feel as though they're fading.

"Yes, he's with her." Johnson's now answering question on Edward's phone.

There's a pause.

"Okay." She answers, ending the call and then speaks to Edward. "Mr Scott, they're on their way."

I try to open my eyes, but the lights are too bright. Johnson's voice sounds panicked. "Your phone, Mr Scott." Edward just grunts at her in response as he holds my head and slowly turns me on my left side. I cry out and tears course down my face. He places his jacket over me, and I can smell his aftershave on it. I feel his rapid breathing on my cheek, his eyes on mine, his hand gently holding my head.

"It hurts, Edward," I whisper.

"Where, Abbie?"

"When I breathe. I'm frightened."

His fingers softly stoke the side of my face, and then his lips touch gently onto mine.

"It's all right, Abbie. Don't talk, sweetheart. Keep still."

But I can hear the worry in his voice and I know it's not all right. He's a doctor, and he knows what's wrong with me.

I feel strange and my skin is so hot. I start muttering, rambling, and try to move Edward's jacket away. I can hear sirens in the distance. The room begins to go dark like before. All the while Edward is talking to me, telling me to, "stay awake."

But I can't. I want to close my eyes and sleep; I want to stop the pain. There's a sudden crash as the doors are flung open. Someone kneels by my side and takes instructions from Edward. My arm is squeezed tightly, and there's a bleeping noise that doesn't stop.

A voice shouts, "Reps thirty-two. Stats eight-five and dropping. Temp, bloody hell, forty-one-point-five."

"Get her on oxygen now – fifteen per cent."

My body starts to shake. Air blasts into my mouth and nostrils, which helps me breathe.

"She's convulsing. Abbie! We need to move her now. Ready?"

"Ready," I hear voices say.

Edward's still shouting instructions as I'm lifted from the floor.

"Strap her in."

I'm being moved rapidly through a door out into the cold. Edward is to the side of me with his hand on my chest. I can't stop shaking. They run down a ramp and into the back of an ambulance. The door shuts abruptly.

"Move it. I'll do her observations on the way. Ring through to A&E. Tell them female, age twenty-six, possible pneumonia, chest X-ray and bloods on arrival."

Edward's voice is different; he seems scared. I feel weird. His voice is so distant. He's pulling on my arm and he's breathing fast while he's talking to me, but I don't know what he's saying – it all sounds jumbled up. Alarms and machines are bleeping. The siren shrieks while Edward snaps at someone in the ambulance. Something sharps enters my arm, making me feel strange. Edward's voice is weird, like he's underwater, then there's blackness.

I come to, hearing more voices and machines alarming. Bright lights sear my eyes.

"Ready? Move."

I slide as I'm pulled to the side. Voices shout back and forth, asking Edward questions.

"Mr Scott, is she taking any medication? Her date of birth, please. Her doctor, her address."

"No, just the pill. April—"

"What date? What year? Is that the contraception pill?"

He flips. "Is there another bloody kind? Get her medical records up and check. April the eighth – she's twenty-six. Work it out."

Then his voice fades and there's silence.

I'm moving again. My arm's being stretched and I feel a sharp scratch.

"Second IV line in."

"Have you done those bloods yet?"

Edward's voice.

"No, Mr Scott."

"Then get them done now, for God's sake. Move out of my way."

There's a scuffle at the side.

Edward's voice is loud and angry. "Give them to me!"

Another voice speaks firmly. "Edward stop; you can't treat her."

"Back off, Bart. Leave me alone. They're incompetent. Look at them – they're wasting time. Have you seen the state of her? Her temp? It's still rising!" His voice is different – shaky, uneasy.

"Edward, you're too emotional. It's not ethical."

"I'm not, and I won't stand aside. You're wasting precious time, Bart – time that she's hasn't got."

He's frightening me. Time I've not got? What does that mean? Oh, Lord, am I dying?

"Edward, please let me take over. Look at your hands – they're shaking."

Edward's breathing hard. I can hear him. He sounds cross, but I think he's moved. His lips are on my forehead. His hand shakes as he strokes the side of my cheek with his fingertips. His voice is soft but firm.

"Come on, Abbie, please … fight this. Come on."

I hear a sharp intake of breath.

"You take over, Bart. But only you, do you hear me? No one else." I can sense the panic.

"I hear you, Edward."

"Now please stand aside."

Muffled words are spoken. My senses are fading again. Silence.

There's something tight on my arm. Another sharp scratch. A feeling of warmth gushing into my veins. Air blasting into my mouth. Numbers are spoken, questions about medication. None of it makes any sense.

I try to move my arm but someone's holding it down. Then more warmth flows up my arm. I want to tell them to stop, that they're hurting me.

Edward asks someone about numbers, and they answer him, but I don't understand what they mean. Then more heat feeds into me, making me feel woozy.

Then blackness again.

I feel fingertips gently stroking the side of my face. I hear a voice I recognise, that makes me feel safe.

"Hey, sweetheart. Open your eyes for me."

I strain to open them, but they won't. I try to talk, but I'm unable to.

He continues to stroke the side of my face.

"Come on, Abbie, try. Try and open your eyes."

I'm trying so hard but they're stuck.

"Alison and Tom have been to see you. And your gran's here, though she's just nipped out for some air. She's been here since Monday."

Monday? What day is it? Oh, my gran. I try to smile, but I feel so sleepy, like my eyes are glued together.

Then sleep comes again.

I look down and I'm confused. What on earth am I wearing?

"No!" I scream.

I'm being dragged down the aisle again. The hand that's pulling me stops, allowing me to break free.

Now I'm running up my stairs at home. I'm panicking. There's blood on my face. I hear footsteps behind me. I run into the bathroom and lock the door.

"Open this fucking door now."

I remember this. He hit me again, knocked me to the floor. No more.

"No," I scream.

The door opens, and he's gone.

I don't understand what's going on.

I hear shouting from the hallway; it's him. God, he's yelling at me. I start to run down the stairs. He's beating me. I don't want to see this – anything but this. But I can't leave knowing what he's doing, and knowing what's about to happen next. I need to help.

I run over to him, screaming, "No. No more. Never again."

I throw myself on top of the vulnerable, petrified person on the floor – me.

Now I'm in my bedroom, staring at myself on the bed. I'm holding on to my stomach, whimpering for my baby. Blood covers the duvet. I close my eyes, not wanting to relive this. Tears course down my face as I watch myself losing my child. He stands at the door with a drunken smirk on his face. I hear him coming up the stairs. I fly out of the room with fury raging through me. I want to hurt him badly.

I grab him and scream, "You leave her alone. You hear me? No more."

I feel utter repulsion for him. I push him backwards. He stumbles and hovers over the banister. Then he begins to fall. I laugh as I see the fear in his eyes. He grabs for my jumper and holds on to it, and we both tumble to the floor. I close my eyes, waiting to hit the ground.

Now Adam's chasing me through a wood that's thick with trees and undergrowth. It's damp and cold. I shiver. It's dark and I can't see very well. I start to run away from him, looking over my shoulder as I go; he's gaining on me and shouting about what he's going to do to me for answering him back. I suddenly trip but scramble to my feet. My heart races as I try to put distance between us.

I stop in my tracks and stare. I hear children's laughter. Their voices are excited, and it's infectious. I smile, curious as to where the sound's coming from. I turn back around and Adam's gone.

I focus on the laughter; it draws me closer. A bright light has appeared, making me squint. I smile again as I see two small silhouettes. They're running around, chasing each other, chuckling as they play. It makes me feel happy and I want to join in. I walk towards them, waving, but they don't see me.

A voice shouts, "There you two are. I've been looking for you everywhere."

I can't take my eyes off them. I'm completely drawn. They stop giggling and run towards her voice. She comes closer and I can see her faintly. She's young, my age. She must be their mummy. They call out to her excitedly.

"Gran, Gran."

She beckons them.

I'm puzzled. Gran? That can't be right; she's too young.

She scoops them both into her outstretched arms. She sees me and smiles. She knows me.

"Abigail, sweetheart, what are you doing here? You can't stay."

A wave of emotion hits me as I recognise the voice. Tears well in my eyes as I stare at her and at the children. It's her, my mother. And those children are my angels, my babies, and they're here with her, safe. Tears fall down my cheeks. I try to run to them. I want to hug them, play with them. But I'm unable to go.

She doesn't want me to.

She's shaking her head at me, mouthing, "Let it go, Abigail."

Then I'm on my knees, begging.

"Please, please let me come with you."

I hear Edward shouting for me.

I'm torn, so torn. I want to hold my babies, laugh with them, kiss and cuddle them.

Now I hear my gran's voice, and I can feel breath on the side of my face; it's a feeling of love and warmth. A voice pleads with me to open my eyes. Edward. He's here. I feel his hand on my shoulder. I turn, smile and nod. I want to say to him, "Look at my babies – they're safe." I turn back around and point. But the light's fading fast and I can't see them anymore.

I turn my head to Edward, still feeling his breath on my face. He whispers into my ear, "Abbie, open your eyes, sweetheart. Please, I need you."

He needs me, but I'm so confused. I need to tell him what I saw, that they were there, I know they were. Strangely, though, I don't feel sad because I know they're with my mother. Safe, happy and loved.

And for the first time, my heart feels at peace.

I try to speak and I can hear my gran's voice.

"Edward, did you see that?" Her voice is surprised, stunned almost. "What did you say to her?"

"What did you see Elizabeth?" he responds, bemused.

"She smiled Edward … she just smiled."

It's growing dark, but I don't want the shadows; I want to wake up.

I feel like there's a hedgehog prickling in my throat which makes me cough. I need a wee desperately. I strain with the effort of trying to move and my head thumps as if there's a pneumatic drill boring through my skull. Hell, now someone's shining a bright light into my eyes. I try to knock it out of the way. It moves and I catch an arm.

"Hello there."

I don't know the voice but I want to tell it to stop. My arm hurts – it's being squeezed so tight I think it's going to fall off. I've no feeling left in my hand or my fingers. Something beeps and the same voice speaks again.

"Hmm, they're all coming back to normal. Temp good. Excellent, she's waking up as well. You'd better bleep Mr Scott, Nurse Beverly."

"Yes, Mr Grant."

Something's removed from my face.

"Abigail, time to start waking up. Nurse Beverly has gone to page Edward, and you know what he's like – he'll expect you to be sitting up in bed when he arrives."

He laughs at his own joke, although I don't really get it. Suddenly, I hear an excited voice.

"Bart, I told you to page me immediately if she woke."

"Edward, she's only barely begun to stir."

"And her gran, does she know?"

"Not yet. Give us a minute, mate."

"A minute. Bloody hell, I've given you enough minutes. She's been out for nearly two days."

"Really? I'd not noticed," he replies sarcastically.

I want to roll my eyes at them, but Nurse Beverly jumps to the rescue.

"Mr Grant, Mr Scott, is this appropriate? I mean in front of Abigail?"

There's silence from them both, then Edward shocks me.

"Thank you for taking care of her, Bart."

"You're welcome. She obviously means a great deal to you."

"That she does."

He sighs, placing his hand on mine, before kissing me gently on the forehead. My eyes flicker at the feel of his lips on my skin.

"Abbie. God, you scared me, girl."

My mouth starts to move into a smile as my senses return. My eyes open and focus. He has the biggest, cheesiest grin on his face.

"Don't you ever do that to me again." He breathes out deeply then bends forward and gently cradles me in his arm, whispering, "Thank God. Are you okay?"

He goes to pull away, but I don't move. I place my arms around him and hold him to me, feeling loved, settled and at peace.

"I'm okay now, thank you. And they're safe."

And I mean every word.

We sit on my hospital bed, holding each other, each with our own thoughts. And, for once, my thoughts are nice ones. My angels are with my mother, and the man I desperately love is here with me. And although he's not told me he loves me, I feel it so very much.

I'm suddenly brought out of my daydream by an excited screech.

"Abbie, you're awake."

I smile over Edward's shoulder. Alison's grinning at me. And behind her is my gran. She's holding her hand to her mouth.

"Abigail!" she says, her voice laced with emotion.

Edward moves to one side as she sits at the side of the bed and gently places her arms around me. I feel overrun with emotion.

"I'm sorry I put you through that, Gran."

She doesn't speak, merely kisses my forehead. And, as always, I can't help what happens next – a tear falls to my cheek. She wipes it, shaking her head.

"I think we've seen enough of these."

"Yes, we have. No more."

"Yes, Abbie, no more."

I close my eyes and hold her – I'm desperate to tell her about my mother and my beautiful angels. Then I open them and stare at Edward. He nods at me. I hold my hand out to him and he takes it.

"I love you," I mouth.

His eyes go wide. I smile, then nod my head. He's dumbstruck, and squeezes my fingers.

"Abbie!" he eventually replies.

Gran takes a deep breath. "Well, Alison, I think we should go for that coffee now."

Alison nods.

I hug my gran the best I can, knowing exactly what she's doing.

"You rest now, Abigail." She bends a little closer to my ear and whispers. "Tell him again, Abbie. He's a good un. Trust me."

I smile and kiss her on the cheek.

"I'll be back in about an hour," she says to Edward. "I'll bring coffee."

"Thank you, Elizabeth."

"You're welcome."

I grin, because this is nice – the two people I love most in the world are here with me and they like each other. Gran thinks he's a good 'un, and I think he is too. No. I *know so.*

They leave the room. Edward is still staring. I smile and pat the bed. As I try to sit against the bedrest, I wince. He instinctively moves to adjust the pillows behind me.

"Here, let me help you up," he says bossily. "Ready?" He places his hands under my arms to help me. "Take a deep breath."

I inhale deeply and he moves me up the bed with ease. "Better?"

"Yes, thank you. Will you now please sit?" I pat the bed.

The atmosphere is a little tense, as neither of us knows quite what to say or who should go first. So I decide to take the lead.

"Edward."

His eyes close, though I'm not sure why. I take a deep breath, wondering whether it was too soon – maybe I've put him on the spot.

He takes me by surprise though. "Abbie, did you mean what you said?"

I nod, dreading what he's going to say.

He takes a deep breath. "Will you say it again?"

I lift my gaze. My heart races.

"Please?" he asks, smiling.

It's a warm, inviting smile. I look into his eyes – they're endearing, captivating. I hold his gaze and his expression is kind, loving and full of tenderness. A feeling of pure emotion surges through me – a mixture of happiness, love and nerves. Because I don't know whether he feels the same.

I take a deep breath. I promised myself I'd never bury my head in the sand again.

"I love you."

He places his arms around me and pulls me gently into them. I snuggle my face into the side of his neck and hold my breath. He pulls away and cups my face in his hands.

He smiles as I look into his eyes, and he breathes deeply. "And I'm falling for you."

Tears come immediately and fall onto my cheeks; I can't stop them. And I don't want to because they feel so different. It's like my heart's just grown fourfold. And I feel changed.

"Hey, what's this?" he asks, wiping the tears from my cheek.

I shrug.

"Are you sad?"

I shake my head.

"Why the tears?"

"Happy tears, Edward."

"Happy tears?"

I nod, and he tilts his head to one side as if he's mulling over my words.

"Happy tears? I can live with happy tears, Abbie."

I inwardly smile, knowing I can too.

We hold each other in silence and I've no doubt what-so-ever that this is where he belongs – here in my heart. And I in his.

I close my eyes and hold him as he lays me down gently, whispering. "Sleep Abbie. You rest, and I'll sit here with you."

And I do. I just close my eyes as he holds my hand. I hear him breathing and I feel his eyes on me. I want to gaze at them but I'm so tired. My eyes are too heavy to stay open but my heart is as light as a feather … and at peace.

And as I slowly drift off into my dreams, it's the most beautiful feeling in the world.

Chapter 3

I wake, startled and embarrassed; I think I've wet the bed I try to sit up and Edward jumps to his feet.

"Hell, what's the matter?" he says, his voice worried.

My face flushes. "Please can you get the nurse, Edward?"

"Why, what's the matter?"

"Please, just get the nurse." I can't tell him the reason; I'm mortified by just the thought of it.

"No, Abbie. Tell me what's wrong. You're scaring me."

I shake my head.

"Do you not feel well?" He starts feeling my face, observing me in a clinical way.

"I'm okay, honestly. I don't feel ill, but please, Edward, just go and get the nurse for me."

He looks puzzled and he's not for shifting. He shakes his head, waiting for me to tell him what's wrong. I close my eyes, knowing he won't go until I've told him. I feel the flush deepen on my cheeks.

"I think I've wet the bed," I whisper.

Relief plays across his face. I'm dumbstruck by his reaction. He laughs quietly and I raise my eyes.

"It's not funny," I say.

He pulls in his lip, trying to contain himself.

"Sorry. No, no it's not funny, but I thought it was something serious. It'll be your catheter, that's all. Let me see."

It's almost a demand, as he lifts the sheets to look. I slap his hand firmly, and he glares at me in shock. But I feel self-conscious. Have I not been through enough these past few weeks? And now I have to endure the humiliation of wetting the bed.

"No, Edward, you're not looking," I reply, my voice raised, so he knows I mean it. He steps back a little from the bed, but still holds the sheet. It's a stalemate.

"Why not?" he says again.

"B-Because" – I pull at the sheet and push his hand away – "you're not!"

"Don't be silly. Let me see. I am a bloody doctor, Abbie," he replies and grabs for the sheet.

"No. Get off. I know you're a bloody doctor, but you're not looking, okay? It's not right."

He laughs, then tilts his head and gives me that boyish grin. Then he raises his eyes and speaks. His voice is soft and low, and I know what he's doing.

"I've seen a little more than that."

"You can stop that right now," I say. My face is crimson.

He smiles cutely and suggestively, and I wonder whether he has any scruples at all. Or is this just him, back to normal, being suggestive? And he does love making me blush. I roll my eyes. "God, I'm in hospital, and my gran is coming back soon. Just go and get the nurse, please, or I'll do it myself."

"Oh, you will, will you?"

I know his game, the bossy little bugger.

"Yes, I will." I poke out my tongue, as he grins, knowing I've busted him, and am on to him.

He gives up and mutters, "Hell, you're one stubborn bloody woman, Abigail!" He shakes his head and walks through the door to get the nurse.

I sit up gingerly on the bed. There's a slight grin on my face; I won that little battle.

I look under the sheets. Thank God, I've not wet the bed, but I do feel desperate to wee. I start moving my bottom, squirming in discomfort.

Edward walks back into the room with Nurse Beverly, who's carrying a dressing pack. She smiles as she speaks.

"Hi, Abbie. Mr Scott as asked me to come and remove the catheter for you. I believe it's causing you some discomfort." I nod. "I'll just wash my hands then, if that's okay. Then we can remove it."

After she's come back from the bathroom, she looks at me and I smile. Then her eyes turn to Edward.

"Oh, are you staying Mr Scott?"

I nearly choke as I answer not giving Edward the opportunity to reply, as I think I know what he'll say.

"No. No he's not." I'm determined he won't stay.

A chuckle leaves his throat, and a small grin appears on his face. He knows he's lost another battle.

"No, I'll wait outside." He looks at me still grinning, and remarks, "I think Abbie's a little embarrassed, Beverly." Then he walks towards the door, turns to me and winks before he leaves.

I sigh with relief. *Embarrassed?* That's the understatement of the bloody year. Beverly just shrugs. She seems a little taken a back but remains professional as she tells me what to do.

"You just need to lie down, Abbie." And I do as she says. "Have you had a catheter before?" I shake my head. "Don't worry – it doesn't hurt when it's being removed. All you'll feel is a little tug, that's all. Generally, they come out pretty quickly. Now, all I need you to do is bend your legs then bring them up towards your bottom; relax them at the knees, and then open them onto the bed."

I nod and go bright red, but do as she asks. She opens the pack and starts to prepare the area, placing a sheet under my bottom. "Everything's ready, Abbie." She smiles as she puts on the gloves, careful not to touch anything. "Are you ready? Take a deep breath and hold it in." I close my eyes and inhale. "Just letting the balloon down, Abbie." I nod, wondering how long I have to lie like this for. I feel completely exposed and vulnerable. There's a little tug. "All done. It's out. That wasn't that bad, was it?"

I shake my head as she replaces the sheet back over me, but now I have a sudden, desperate urge to wee.

"Beverly, sorry, could you help me to the bathroom, please?

"Yes, of course."

She helps me to sit. I wobble a little so she places her arm around me and helps me to stand. "I'll walk in with you – you seem a little unsteady."

We enter the bathroom and she helps me to sit on the toilet. "Please ring the nurse-call when you've finished. I'm just going to clear up in there."

"Thank you, I will."

"Good, because I don't want a telling-off from Mr Scott if you fall." She pulls a mock grimace as she leaves the bathroom.

I wee, and wee, and wee, thinking it's never going to stop, but feel so much better when I'm done. I try to stand but stumble, so I press the nurse-call for Beverly. She comes in just a second later.

"Finished?"

"Yes, thank you."

She helps me to stand and then guides me to the sink to wash my hands.

"Beverly, can I ask you something?" She nods. "What did you mean when you said you'd get told off by Mr Scott? ...

Has he been bossy?" She just raises her eyes, and that confirms it. I shake my head. "What's he done?"

She smiles at me. "Well, I suppose he's been a little bossy, but in a really kind way. Towards you, I mean."

"Me?"

She nods. "I shouldn't say anything really, but it was so sweet. We all said so. Even Mr Grant."

I'm puzzled and intrigued. "What was sweet?"

"Mr Scott. He wouldn't leave you. Insisted on washing you, brushing your hair, turning you, applying cream to your bruises, because he didn't want you to get sore. And when he'd done all that to make sure you were comfortable, he showered in there." She points to the bathroom. I notice a toiletry bag on the shelf that must be his, and feel warmth and hope inside me. She continues in a soft voice. "And then he went off to work."

I pull my lip in tight, closing my eyes, not believing he did all that for me. When I open them Beverly is nodding; I think she can see what's going on in my head – it must be written all over my face.

"Then he came back at lunch time, read to you, never stopped talking to you. He played music, then went back to work. When he'd finished, he came back and started all over again." "Wow," I whisper, as we walk back into my room. Beverly continues to nod telling me about this beautiful man who genuinely cares for me.

"Yes. Wow. That's what we all thought. And, to be honest, we were all a little jealous."

"Why?"

"I think it's rare to have love like that, genuine love."

I can't speak because I can't describe what her words mean to me. What she told me about Edward, what he's done. She points to the chair and my eyes follow.

"And he slept in that chair every night. He wouldn't leave – wanted to be here when you woke up."

I stare at the chair, knowing that he's been with me every night, waiting for me to wake.

The words I croak are laced with affection. "He did?"

"Yes, Abbie, he did."

Edward walks back into the room, smiling. There are no tell-tale signs of what he's done, no hint of the sacrifice he's made over the past few days. Just his usual self-confident, I'm-in-charge manner. But I know different. He's Edward Scott, my Edward Scott. Caring, loving, and so endearing that I can't help but fall in love with him.

"Thank you. I'll take her from here," he says to Beverly, his voice resonant with authority. Beverly just smiles. He places his arm gently around my waist and guides me towards the bed. I just breathe evenly, knowing he's keeping his promise to look after me. And, boy, has he looked after me. That's why Gran said he was a good' un. I smile at him, and he winks as he lifts me gently back onto the bed. And I let him, because he's more than a good 'un. A little bossy, but now I know that it's for all the right reasons, and that makes one hell of a difference.

"How are you, my little stubborn—"

I stop him in his tracks with a kiss to the lips.

"Mmm, better it seems. Please don't stop."

So I don't. I kiss him long and deep as he holds me gently to him, and I don't ever want to stop, although I have to as someone enters the room and coughs.

"Well, you two, it looks like you need a chaperone," my gran says, her voice echoing in the silence between us. We both look at her, then at each other, and grin. I'm suddenly hit by a waft of something delicious. I inhale deeply looking back towards her.

"Gran, have you been to the deli?" She nods. "And have you brought make-better soup?"

She laughs.

Edward appears confused. "Make-better soup?"

"Yes. Smell." He sniffs as I continue, "when I was a little girl, Gran always made her to-die-for chicken soup if I was poorly – to make me better. And since then we've always called it—"

Gran laughs. And together we say, "Make-better soup."

Edward smiles while Gran holds out a cup for him.

"Would you like to try some, Edward?"

We finish the soup and I yawn.

"Tired, Abbie?" Edward asks. I nod as he speaks to my gran. "Elizabeth, that was to die for. You should markct that."

Gran just raises her eyes at him. Little does he know she already has, but she replies modestly, "Thank you."

"You lie down, Abbie," he says as I yawn again. "Get some sleep. Bart might let you home later on today if you do as you're told."

So I do. I close my eyes. I'm very sleepy, and wonder whether my gran drugs her soup.

I hear them talking and it's a lovely feeling to hear them laughing quietly together.

I'm just nodding off to sleep when Edward says, just loud enough that I can hear him, "Elizabeth, the police have been on the phone again."

I go to speak, then stop myself, knowing that if I interrupt him he'll not continue. But I'm too inquisitive so I keep my eyes closed and listen in silence.

"Did they say what they were going to do – about Adam?" Gran asks.

"Yes." His voice is a little louder.

"What?"

"Nothing."

"Nothing? You're kidding. After what he's done? All the things he's done to her, and they're going to do nothing? Why?"

Fear and dread have risen through me. Gran sounds annoyed, and I'm praying he's not told her everything that was said in the interview room at the police station. I know it would crush her. And he promised me. *Whatever's said stays within those four walls.*

He sighs heavily. "They said they had no proof, because there was no phone, and no witness to the Saturday night."

I sigh with relief, knowing she doesn't know the whole truth, the depravity, the lengths to which Adam went too, to hurt me. They've stopped talking, and I presume they're both looking at me. I want to open my eyes and fight; tell them he's not getting away with what he's done. I should've been stronger before but I wasn't, and I never reported the other things either. I told them at the hospital that I'd fallen. Although they knew different. But that's what I said, too scared to say anything else. But that doesn't mean I'm not strong enough now, because I am. He thinks he's so clever, but I've learned something these past weeks – if I set my mind to something, I can be better than him, because bullies always get their comeuppance in the end. What's the saying – *Karma's a bitch.* Well, he ain't seen this angry bitch yet. And I *am* angry, so angry with him.

"I'll sort this, Elizabeth. Trust me. He's not getting away with it. I've spoken to Simon again, and he's doing some digging on him."

I wonder who Simon is.

"Will he not get into trouble for doing that?" Gran asks. "What rank is he?"

"Chief inspector."

"Really? Well, that's good." She sounds pleased.

"Yes, it is, because if anyone can do some digging its Simon. I've told him everything that's happened, and he's more than annoyed that Adam's been able to get away with it – even more so that the man's used his standing as a solicitor and twisted events to exonerate himself. He's been very cunning, and, to be honest with you, Elizabeth, I'd not be surprised if these past four years were premeditated."

"Premeditated? What do you mean?"

There's a growing silence in the room, but I think I know what Edward means. Gran, though, seems rather baffled, and that's probably down to the fact that I've never told her the truth about the miscarriages. When you add everything up – and Edward does now know everything – I think he's right. He married me for my money, nothing else, and babies would have taken that money away from him. Could that have been his motive? I feel sick at the thought that someone could be so immoral as to knowingly do that to another human being. But I can't prove it – that he played mind games with me, which caused me to miscarry my first baby, or that he hit me until I miscarried the second. He would never incriminate himself, like that. Never. I'm going to have to be cleverer than him. I'm going to have to catch him out.

Gran breaks the stretching silence.

"But … Abigail left him?"

Edward's quiet. I think he knows he's said to much and is trying to throw her off the scent.

"Sorry. Perhaps premeditated is the wrong word. It's just that I'm angry and upset." His response sounds convincing.

"Hmm, yes, of course you are. It's only natural, dear. We both are."

I breathe lightly, hoping that Gran doesn't ask any further questions.

"It's very good of you to involve your brother. I do really appreciate it," she says, changing the subject.

I'm not at all convinced she believes him; she's not stupid and I wonder whether she knows a lot more than she's admitting too, although she lets it go for now.

"You're welcome. I want him out of Abbie's, life, and sent down for what he's done." I hear a sharp intake of breath. "Have you thought about what I asked you?"

"Yes, I have, and there's nothing I'd like more than for Abigail to come home with me so I can look after her. But I'm sure you can look after her equally well. And I'm sure she'd like to go home with you."

"I know. That's how I feel. But, you see, I promised Abbie I'd take care of her, and I never go back on my promises," he says quietly. And I can tell that he means it.

"I can see why she likes you so much, Edward. That was a sweet thing to say. That's something her …" She breathes out. "Her grandad would have said." And I can hear the love in her voice.

Edward doesn't respond, and I know why – he's probably a little taken aback. I know I am. And I would like to go to Edward's because it'll give us time to get to know each other properly, and I'll feel safe with him. I always do.

They continue to discuss my future as I drift off to sleep.

I wake and yawn.

"Well, hello, you! You've been asleep for quite some time. How are you feeling?" says Edward.

"A lot better, thank you. And the pain's gone. I just feel sleepy all the time."

"Good, because if you're up to it, Bart has said you can go home."

I raise my eyes slightly. *Home?*

He notices my reaction, and rephrases his sentence. "Well, he actually said he'd discharge you, but only into my capable hands," he says confidently, as though Bart really had said those words.

I smile. "Only into your capable hands, Mr Scott. Nobody else's?"

He winks, trying not to laugh.

"No, just mine, Abbie, and only mine."

"Well, how can a girl refuse an offer like that?" I grin as he raises his eyebrows. Is he wondering what I'm going to say next? So I nod my head in confirmation, and cough lightly. "In your capable hands I am, then, Mr Scott."

It's him that nods this time, like he always does when he gets his own way. Then, with that air of overconfidence in his voice, he bats back, "Quite right too, Abbie. Nobody does it better."

I shake my head, and knocking his shoulder playfully. "Shut up! Who do you think you are, James Bond?"

He laughs again, quite loudly this time. "Play your cards right and you can be my Miss Moneypenny."

"Oh dear, this conversation is going very wrong for a hospital ward."

"Shall we continue it at home then?" he says, smirking.

"Mmm, that sounds like a better idea."

I look down at the gown I'm wearing. "but I'll need some clothes."

He lifts a small brown leather holdall from the floor.

"While you were asleep, Alison brought you some of her things to wear."

"But you could've brought me something of my own from my bags. The ones I had at the hotel. Aren't they still in the car?" I ask.

"They are, but Tom drove back to the house to pick up some clean shirts and stuff I needed for work. And, anyway, we needed to change the car because of the weather. Your bags are still in the BM."

I smile, knowing that what Beverly said is true – he'd stayed here all the time with me, not left the hospital even for a change of clothes.

"Alison said you're the same size." He smiles at me. "You don't mind, do you?"

"No, honestly. Alison's things will be fine. You seem to have thought of everything, Edward."

He smiles, pleased with himself.

"Come on. Let's get you dressed. And no arguments this time."

But I've no intention of arguing this time, because I rather like being looked after.

So I just smile and say. "Okay."

He looks shocked. "No, come back, Abbie."

I just shake my head.

Chapter 4

I'm dressed and sit on the bed in a pair of Alison's jeans, a jumper, boots and underwear, waiting for Edward to return to my room. He's gone to bring the car around to the front of the hospital. There's a knock at the door, and Nurse Beverly enters, pushing a wheel chair.

I shake my head. "Really? Do I have to?"

"I'm afraid so. Sorry. Somebody insisted."

I raise my eyes, and she smiles.

Edward's back and has heard the conversation, he makes that clear as he coughs to get my attention. "It's either that or I carry you." He remarks meaning every single word.

I just roll my eyes at him knowing he probably would. "Okay, I'll sit."

We leave the ward and he places his coat over me as he pushes me along the corridor to the main entrance.

"It's cold outside, Abbie. It's been snowing."

"Really?" I say, full of enthusiasm. "I love snow. There's something magical about it, don't you think?" I turn my head around to see him, but he merely smiles.

It's freezing cold. Snow covers the ground. He pushes me over to an impressive black four-wheel-drive Range Rover. I shake my head, and he gives me a boyish grin that nearly melts my heart let alone the snow.

"What, Abbie?" he answers with a smile I think knowing what I'm about to say to him.

"Car number three?" I murmuring. "Boys and their toys!"

He opens the door and the warmth hits me, making my cold cheeks tingle. I smile inwardly, and look at him as he holds out his hands to help me from the chair and lifts me gently onto the seat. I bend forward as he reaches over me to fasten my seat belt. I cup his face in my hands as I gently kiss him on the lips, knowing all these little things – him helping me, washing me, staying with me, leaving the heating on in the car – mean so much to me, because they mean he cares. And sometimes it's the little things in life that count so much. To someone else they might seem like nothing, but to me they mean the world because I've never experienced them other than from my gran.

"Thank you," I whisper.

He fastens my seat belt, and continues to fuss over me until he's happy. Then he throws the brown holdall onto the back seat and returns the wheelchair to the hospital entrance. I sit and stare at him as he walks back to the car. I can't seem to stop smiling. He jumps spritely into driver's side and winks.

"Home, Abbie?"

I nod, holding my emotions in "Home!" I reply happily.

I feel exhausted, and I've only got dressed, but happy, ever so happy that we're here, and finally together.

I yawn and watch him driving.

"Sleepy?" he asks. I nod. "Then close your eyes. It's about twenty minutes to the cottage."

I'm shattered. The car is warm and snuggly. I drift off to sleep thinking, *Edward lives in a cottage?* I hadn't expected that. Maybe a penthouse, or a luxury harbour pad, but not a cottage. And I realise we really don't know anything about each other at all. I close my eyes still smiling at the thought of Edward's home. He's full of surprises.

I wake as the Range Rover turns the corner onto a bumpy road lined with what I can only describe as mansions. Long drives wind through beautiful gardens. I notice a sign that reads "Private road". I look at Edward, surprised.

"Hi. You're awake. Not far now – the cottage is just at the end."

"Portland Drive, eh?" I tease.

"You know it?"

"Oh, yes. I deliberated over a house once – overlooking the golf course – but then I thought, nah! Eight bedrooms – is that all? Are you serious? Portland Drive? I thought you had to have an off-shore bank account to live here." He grins as he slows the Range Rover and turns onto an unmade road.

"Not quite Portland Drive, Abbie."

My eyes nearly pop out of my head as we reach the top of the road.

"Really? A cottage, Edward?" I remark astounded.

He laughs and unassumingly points to a sign at the entrance of the gated drive.

"That's what the sign says – The Old Cottage," he bats back with a hint of sarcasm.

"I'd say the sign is a little modest, given the size of the cottage."

The cottage is double-fronted. A huge old oak door stands in the middle with two large windows either side. Five equally large windows are on the first floor – there must be at least seven or eight bedrooms in the place. The thatched roof is spectacular; scalloped ridges overhang each window, cut and shaped immaculately.

I smile, thinking, *That's Edward. Modest as ever.* A cottage, he'd said. I was expecting a small picket-fence job, not a huge manner house that wouldn't look out of place in a Dickens novel. All the things he's done; the books he's written … he never brags about any of it.

He opens his window and punches a number into the keypad. The gates open onto a tree-lined gravel drive that bends and sweeps through the grounds to the entrance.

"It's stunning, Edward. How old is it?"

He points to a sign above the door that I can just make out as we drive up.

"1703. Wow."

He's got that grin again on his face. I'm stunned by the magnificence of the place.

"You like it?" he asks.

"It's okay, I suppose." I turn to him, shaking my head. "I'm just a little worried. 1703. So no plumbing, then."

"No, Abbie." He smirks and tries not to laugh. "Sorry – that's the downside. A bucket for night-time and a hole in the garden during the day."

I look at him with disappointment.

"Oh dear. I think I better go back to the hospital. I mean … it's a bit chilly for buckets and holes, don't you think?"

He bursts out laughing.

"Oh, Abigail, where is your sense of adventure, girl?"

I shrug. "Okay. I'll try it for one night, but if I get frostbite, I'm off in the morning."

"Deal."

He winks and I feel so relaxed as we continue towards the entrance. I stare, speechless again, as we pass laurel topiary that's been clipped into all sorts – there's a fox, a pheasant, a peacock. All these twisting shapes – they're magnificent.

I giggle. "Edward, are these the products of those nimble fingers of yours?"

"I'm afraid not, dear. They are, in fact, the workings of my nimble-fingered gardener, Jimmy. Talented, isn't he?"

"Very!"

The rest of the grounds are laid mainly to lawn. They appear to wrap around the entire building. Borders section off areas with large shrubs and trees, although I can't see much as there's a blanket of snow covering the ground. Surrounding the grounds is a twelve-foot-high weathered red-brick wall. To the right of the cottage, I can see two outbuildings and something behind one of them.

"What are they used for, Edward?"

He points at the first one. "That one I use for my cars. The second is a stable block. And behind the stable block, down a path, is Jimmy's lodge house. He lives on the grounds."

So it's an estate. My eyes glance back towards the stable block. I'm a little nervous.

"You have horses, Edward?"

"Yes, Abbie, I have horses. Do you ride?"

I shake my head. Then I imagine Edward on a horse and grin to myself. Mmm, now that would be a sight for sore eyes.

"No, I don't. In fact, I'm a little scared of them."

"Nonsense. I'll teach you to ride," he says bossily.

I don't reply, hoping he'll forget about it. I glance out of the window, and notice two topiary swans looking at each other with their beaks touching; they look magical with a dusting of snow on them. Edward notices me looking as he applies the brakes and pulls the car to a stop. He gets out, walks over to my side and opens the door. "They mate for life," he says softly.

I just smile at him, wondering whether he's talking about swans or himself.

"Here, take my arm."

He's so thoughtful. I reach up and kiss him on the lips.

"Thank you."

"For what?"

"For everything – this, you, just everything."

"You're sweet, Abbie. Come on – it's cold and you need to be in bed, resting."

I can't take my eyes off him. I want to prick myself with a pin to see if I'm dreaming. I'm struggling to contain the emotions running through me and the feelings I have for him. Might he really feel the same? I hope so. I want him to. I want to love him for the rest of my life, but most of all I want him to love me for the rest of his life. I want us to be like those two swans at the front door, mating for life, in love and happy for eternity.

Edward unlocks the front door. It opens with a creek, and I'm blown away by the large hall that greets me.

"Edward, it's beautiful."

"Here." He points towards an ottoman that's to one side against the wall.

"Sit a minute, Abbie." I do but it's not that comfortable. "I just need to do something. Would you wait here for me, please?"

I nod. He walks down one of two hallways and disappears through a door at the end.

I look around. Across from me is an oak fire surround, about six or seven feet tall. The wood is beautifully polished. On the back panel above the mantel is a bevelled mirror. Through it I can see a stained-glass window that illustrates a church. The sun outside is low in the sky and shines through the window. The mirror acts like a prism, bouncing blues, reds, greens and yellows onto the white walls. I watch as the colours dance and flicker around. The effect is hypnotic.

The black cast-iron fireplace is surrounded by cream-coloured tiles that look to be hand-painted with red poppies. One of my favourite flowers. There are logs in the grate, but it's not lit. I smile as I see a bronze of a lone stallion, about a foot high, sitting proudly off centre on the mantelpiece. And then I feel sad, imagining this to be Edward. A lone stallion with no mate.

The floor is oak, very old, and the floorboards are wide. An expensive thick rug sits in the centre of the large entrance area. A sweeping staircase appears to lead to numerous rooms, though I can't be sure from where I'm sitting. It's impressive – the treads are oak and the rails and banister are a flawless white. It screams elegance and country estate, not cottage. The layout is a little like mine at home, but on a far grander scale. It looks homely, inviting.

Edward shouts from the end of the hallway. "Are you still sitting, Abbie?"

"Yes," I reply, intrigued.

"Go on then, Shadow."

I smile as I see the most beautiful dog skidding towards me.

"Slowly, Shadow!" Edward says as he approaches me.

The dog eases up then sits looking at Edward, waiting for his next command.

"Okay, Shadow. Say hello. Nicely."

The dog sniffs the air and comes towards me. He's gorgeous – all furry and cuddly. Edward sits down beside me.

"Hold your hand out to him. Let him sniff you."

I do so. Shadow sniffs my hand.

"Can I stroke him?" I'm dying to cuddle this huge ball of fur in front of me.

"Yes, now you've met and he knows you're a friend."

"Hello, boy," I say, stroking him behind the ear, and he tilts his head to one side and pushes his weight towards my hand.

"He seems to like you."

I giggle. "He has good taste! He's beautiful."

Edward pats Shadow on the back.

The dog turns looking at him, and I can see the bond between them.

"But I think he likes you a lot more."

Edward just pats him again.

"Come on, boy. Let's show Abbie the bedroom."

He stands and raises his eyes in that familiar way. Shadow jumps up and starts making his way to the stairs, wagging his tail and waiting for Edward to follow him.

"Really, Edward. I bet you say that to all the girls."

There's a smirk on my face but his reply surprises me.

"You're the first girl who's ever met Shadow, and the first, might I add, that I've brought here."

I pull in my lip. I think I've offended him.

"I'm sorry. I didn't mean—" Then I remember what Alison told me – that he took his one-night stands back to Tom's after a night out. And, yes, he'd admitted he'd taken them to The Drake. So, if I'm honest, I did mean something by what I just said. Perhaps it's jealously, but then I see his face and I feel special, knowing that I'm the first girl he's brought to his house. And maybe it shows, because he smiles and lets out a huge sigh, and I can't help but wonder if I baffle him with the things I say. I pull a silly face by way of an apology.

"Come on. Let's get you upstairs and settled in bed."

I tut. "Really, Edward? I'd love to see the rest of the house; it's so beautiful."

"Yes," he says firmly. "You can have a tour when you're better. I told Bart I'd look after you. By rights, you should still be in hospital. They only allowed you home with me because I was adamant."

"Okay." I know there's no point in arguing with him as it's probably true, but he still looks shocked.

"Really? No fight?"

"No. No fight, Edward. I'm too tired." I let out a yawn. I'm exhausted. "Take me to bed then," I whisper, and a dark smile plays over his face.

"Oh, I wish I could!" he says huskily.

I smile as he walks over to me with his arms outstretched. I move into them and he holds me gently in his arms. I rest my head on his chest, close my eyes, and inhale deeply.

"I wish you could too, Edward." And I mean every single word.

"Can you manage the stairs or do you want me to carry you?"

"Yes, I can manage the stairs. I feel so much better. I'm just tired, that's all. But thank you."

He takes hold of my hand and leads me towards the staircase. We pass the stallion on the mantle and I run my hand over it, smiling. Edward looks puzzled, but I just smile back at him, thinking, *He's not alone now. I'm here, and I'm his mate.*

We walk up together. There must be at least twenty-five steps; there's a turn in the middle.

We reach the top and stop. He kisses me on the forehead then lifts me into his strong arms. One goes under my legs, the other around my waist, and he cradles me like a child to his chest. I'm shocked at first, but then it reminds me of the first time he picked me up.

"Hey, I can walk, you know," I say softly, but liking it really.

He laughs loudly, and Shadow barks.

"I know you can, but I want to carry you."

"I don't need wrapping up in cotton wool, Edward."

"Oh, but I think you do, Abigail."

I sigh and give up.

"You're daft."

He winks as I gently kiss him on the lips and rest my head into the side of his neck. He carries me along the landing and stops at one of the doors. He opens it takes me into a bedroom. Shadow sits on guard as he places me on the bed.

"There's a fantastic view of the ocean!" He points to a large picture window with French doors that lead onto a balcony.

"Am I allowed to get up and have a look?" I ask, tongue in cheek.

His eyes raise, then he nods and takes my hand.

We walk to the doors. Edward places his arm around my shoulder and points through the glass.

"Can you see the lighthouse in the distance?"

My eyes follow his finger, past the grounds off the cottage, over the brick wall and to the vast grassed area and the ocean beyond. I see the breakwater rocks and the red-and-white lighthouse on the edge of a peninsula.

"Yes. It's magnificent here, Edward. How long have you lived here?"

"About five years." I looking at him while he's talking. He runs his hand up and down my back, gently caressing me. "Although it did need a lot of renovating to bring it up to date inside. The gardens were overgrown. You could tell the house had been impressive but it needed a lot of TLC to bring it up to scratch." He smirks, then chuckles. "A bit like you, Abbie."

"Charmed, I'm sure. Is that how you see me, Edward? A little overgrown?" I'm more than a little shocked.

"No, Abbie. I see beauty that needs TLC to flourish."

I'm taken aback. I wasn't expecting that. Wow. TLC – well, he's certainly showing me plenty of that. God, I could get used to this so easily; he makes me feel warm and settled inside, like I've known him all my life. We bounce so easy off each other, make one another smile and laugh at the things we say and do.

"I'm flattered, Mr Scott," I reply, blushing. "If you continue with these wonderful compliments, I may just have to—" I realise what I was about to say, and my face has gone bright red. *Marry you.* Those are the words I stopped myself saying. Hell, that's taken me by surprise. I change the subject quickly. "It must be nice waking up to a view like that every morning."

"Hmm, it must be!" he says, winking at me as he continues stroking my back, and I know what he's thinking. "Come on. Let's get you into bed. You look shattered."

He gets me comfortable and places a soft cream throw over me. He kisses me on the forehead.

"Sleep, Abbie – that's the best medicine for you. I'm going to make you something to eat. Anything in particular you'd like?"

I shake my head. I'm sick of being in bloody bed and of feeling so tired.

But I reply, "Anything will be fine, Edward. Thank you."

He smiles. "Come, boy," he says to Shadow, who bounds out of the room with him.

I am shattered though. I look around the large room. The bed is huge, and very comfortable; it stands in the middle of the room and I can see the view of the ocean. There are two enormous wardrobes with a dressing table in the middle – all antique furniture and all in oak. The walls, the carpet and the bed linen are all in cream. It looks immaculate – a little sparse but elegant.

One solitary painting hangs on a wall in a large ornate brass frame, portraying what I think is a street in Italy. Possibly the Riviera. I've seen something like it before in the travel agent's or a magazine. Houses are laid to both sides of the narrow cobbled street. Each house is alternately painted pink, yellow or light green. Hanging baskets over the doorways are crammed full of colourful flowers that trail and over-spill down the walls and over the doors.

My eyes follow the street downwards to an old drystone wall, then on to the most breath-taking view I've ever seen. The cliff face is covered in olive and lemon trees that lead down to the ocean.

As my lids close I wonder whether it's real or from someone's imagination. There's a faint signature, but I can't make it out as I drift off. I've never seen anything as captivating or beautiful. I feel happy and contented and I wonder: am I changing? Could I possibly be chasing my own dreams? Is Edward my fate, my destiny, my hope, my happy ever after?

I smile and fall asleep.

Chapter 5

I'm sitting on the dry stone wall, looking out to sea. I inhale deeply as the sweet scent of lemons floods my senses. The view is breath-taking as I watch a little dingy bobbing up and down on the tranquil sea, then lazily stretch out my arms. I feel sleepy and smile to myself as the sun warms my skin. It's so peaceful and quiet.

I suddenly look away, disturbed by music coming from a van that's rattling down the cobbles in front of me. It reminds me of the ice-cream vans at home. Front doors start to open as women of all shapes and sizes leave their houses and approach the van. It's not selling ice-cream but freshly baked bread, and it smells delicious. I think back to being a little girl at the deli, making bread with my gran and grandad. The women are busily chatting to each other as they form a queue at the window of the little blue van. The baker sticks his head out of the window and shouts to a very attractive woman.

'Ciao, Bella!' He waves his arms, beckoning her to come to the window. She smiles back at him and answers, but I don't hear her words. The women move to one side as she approaches the window, and he passes her a loaf of bread.

"Grazie," she replies, blushing.

'Mia Bella, amore … mia Bella,' he replies firmly with one hand on his heart. I smile, not understanding the line, but I know it's nice because she blushes from head to toe, and all the other women in the queue make a cooing noise.

"Ciao, bello," she replies.

He nods, and they both smile.

I wrinkle my nose, thinking, *Aw, they're in love*, and Edward comes to mind and I wonder where he is.

She turns and starts walking away, waving at the baker.

The women are returning to their houses. As he drives away, he calls, "Ciao. Ci vediamo domani."

And waves back. I don't understand the words. *See you tomorrow*, perhaps?

The street is silence again, and I return my eyes to the sea. A refreshing breeze drifts over me, cooling my skin. The olive groves are starting to rustle as the gentle wind passes through the branches. Small waves break onto the beach and the dingy bobs up and down faster in the waves. I feel calm as I inhale the sweet scent.

I'm distracted by the sound of giggling. It makes me smile and I turn my head towards it. Two small children run down the step street shouting, "Mummy, Mummy." I look around to see who they're shouting to, but there's nobody here, only me on the drystone wall.

I'm puzzled and stare at them. They look straight at me, and run towards me, still shouting. Something begins to grow inside me, a feeling I've only experienced once before – in my dream when I saw them with my mother. I gasp as they come closer. And the tears come, because I know it's them. I fling my arms out wide and they run into them. I'm consumed by emotion I can't control. Tears stream down my face as I hold them to me and kiss them.

"Why are you crying?" they ask, but I can't speak. I just pull them close to my heart. They giggle and hug me back. My heart is racing. I'm holdings my babies, my two angels in my arms. The love I feel is nothing more than sublime. I close my eyes, wanting never to let go. They'll disappear again – I know they'll have to go – but not just yet. They're here in my arms for the very first time, and I whisper, "I love you. I love you so much."

My eyes are still closed and I feel them drifting away from me. "Please don't go. Please don't leave me again," I beg as I try to hold on.

"Granma's calling us," they say quietly. One puts its little hand onto my cheek. My heart stops, and I open my eyes, wanting to see my mother again, but she's not here, and I can't hear her calling to them.

"Please, please stay with me."

But they shake their heads innocently and move away from me, and I know they can't stay because they're not of my world.

And then just as suddenly as they appeared, they're gone. I desperately want them to come back, but I know they can't. They came to say goodbye. She sent them. I wipe my tears. I know I'll not see them again. I hug myself, still feeling their little bodies and hands hugging me, their lips on my cheek, and that gentle touch I'll never ever forget. And I weep. I miss them so much. I know one day we'll meet again; until that day arrives, I'll treasure these precious moments I've had with them. I smile towards heaven and thank God and my mother for allowing me this most beautiful gift, one that will be imprinted on my heart for all eternity. I savour the feeling as happy, ever-so-happy tears fall once more onto my cheeks.

"Hey, sweetheart. Why are you crying?" I feel something being moved out of my arms. "Come on, Abbie. Let go of the pillow. Let me see your face. What's wrong?"

I hear something being put down to the side of me; I think it's a tray. I smell fresh bread and lemons and the side of my face being stroked.

I'm awake and hugging a pillow tightly. I shake my head at Edward, not wanting to let go of it, because it feels like I'm still hugging them. He places another gentle kiss on my cheek, and I sob. I still refuse to open my eyes, because I know it was dream, a wonderful, beautiful dream, and I want it to last just a little longer. I know it was the pillow I was hugging, and

Edward kissing me, his gentle touch on my cheek, but I want to pretend it was them just one last time.

I wonder why I dream of them. This is the second time, and it's nice, but so confusing when I wake. I'm scared I'm having a breakdown, afraid to tell Edward in case he thinks I'm crazy. Because although I can sort of rationalise it, deep down I do believe I saw them, hugged them, and that they love me just as much as I love them.

I slowly open my eyes to see him staring at me, bemused as to why I'm sobbing. He lifts the pillow, and I look away from him. He places his hand gently to my face, turning my head towards him.

"Please, Abbie, don't ever turn away from me. Talk to me. Don't bottle things up again. We promised each other. Remember what we said – no secrets."

I nod.

"No matter how hard, or how bad something might be, I want you to tell me … please."

I lower my head and he lifts my chin again, holding my stare. And it's intense but different, new, as if he's looking deep beyond my shattered heart, past my desperate soul, searching and willing me to speak. His smile freezes my heart as I know I'm going to tell him what I've been dreaming about. I take a deep breath and begin.

He sits and listens, absorbing each and every word, as I tell him about holding my children, seeing my mother, and the difference I now feel inside.

"Edward, you …" He stares at me, waiting for me to carry on. "You don't think I'm going mad, do you?" He shakes his head. "Well, why do you think I'm dreaming like this?"

He smiles and touches the side of my face, and his touch is warm and kind.

"You're mending, Abbie."

"Mending?"

He nods. "Yes, mending." He breathes in deeply and speaks his next words softly. "Remember I told you once that you were worth mending?" I nod, listening intently. "Well, that's what's happening; your heart is finally finding peace."

I try hard to hold my tears back. Is this true? Am I finally mending? Can my heart finally find peace?

He smiles with so much love that I can almost see it.

"You think I am?"

He nods then cups my face gently, and stares into my eyes.

"Yes, Abbie, you are."

My lips start to turn upwards into a smile.

"Thank you. Thank you so much for helping me."

I feel changed, empowered, and I know why. It's because I know my babies are safe and with my mother. They forgive me, and they love me. And I love them, and Edward. And although he's not told me he loves me, I know he does because I feel it.

"Shush," he whispers drawing me towards him, as though he's just read my thoughts.

A tingle spreads through my body, igniting every nerve, pumping every vein. I remember the night we made love. I pull him closer until I can feel the rapid breathing of his passion. My breasts graze his chest and he takes my mouth fully as his hand cups one and fondles it firmly. I moan with pleasure.

"Please, Edward, make love to me," I whimper.

He stands me up. He has that same desirous look in his eyes as I have. This is what I what. What we both need. To release the hunger, we have for each other.

He places his thumb into the waistband of my jeans, then tugs, forcing me to move forward between his open legs. His hand slowly moves down between my legs. I moan, pushing forward, and am rewarded as he applies pressure.

"You like that?" I nod. "Good." He presses more firmly and I gasp. "So responsive, Abbie. Take them off … now!" he commands, moving his hand.

I open the button, then the zip. His eyes watch my every move as I slide my jeans down my legs, and step out of them. He pulls me back into his arms.

He growls then stands and grabs my hand placing it on him. "Feel me, Abbie. This is what you do to me."

My heart pounds as my eyes move to his. My pulse is racing, my face scarlet. He breathes in sharply, then spins me around quickly and pulls me into his back. His hand slides up my body towards my breasts. I squirm, wanting him to touch me.

"Please." I roll my hips against him, enticing him. His hands move up my jumper into my bra, and over my breast. I whimper as his fingertip strokes my nipple. His breath floats over my skin, making me break out in goosebumps, and I moan in sweet bliss.

His hand moves to the waist band of my panties. His fingers slide slowly across me, teasing me as I waiting for that touch of intimacy. He moans, sending shivers right through me. He cups me between my legs and I nearly scream with desire.

"Shush …" he whispers, sliding a finger under the material, stroking me, as groan of satisfaction leaves his lips. "You're soaking, Abbie. For me?"

I nod panting softly. I jolt as he inserts a finger, slowly but firmly. My hips roll with the excitement that's building inside of me. His fingers move in deep.

"That's it, Abbie. Let go. Come for me."

I start to tingle, and moan, "yes" as I lose myself in him once more.

My body begins to stiffen, and I know I'm going to orgasm.

"I'm going to fuck you senseless," he rasps.

A whimper leaves my throat as he slides my panties down over my hips. His mouth nips at my ear.

"Bend over."

I comply and he moans. "Exquisite, Abbie."

I swallow, waiting in anticipation, my bottom pressed firmly onto him. I hear his zip being pulled, then jeans and boxers being removed. His hands take my hips and his voice is low and gravelly, "This is going to be fast and quick, Abbie."

I don't want it any other way. I want to release this craving.

He pushes into me deeply and slowly. My eyes roll, and my body feel as if it's going to explode with excitement.

He pulls my jumper up my back and over my head then thrusts into me again. I almost squeal with delight. Because I want him, all of him; I'm past the point of no return. I scream in ecstasy as I'm climaxing hard. My legs shake and I nearly fall to the floor. He holds me around my waist, pulling out of me and turning me fast to face him. His face is consumed with lust, hungry to have me again.

He steps back and sits on the bed, holding himself.

"Fuck me, Abbie," he growls, propping himself against the headboard. I straddle him and he sinks into me again. The feeling is out of this world. I lean forward into his chest and move slowly, whimpering in ecstasy.

I watch his face. His eyes roll and I know he's orgasming. I push hard onto him, feeling my own body climaxing again.

"I'm coming, baby."

I keep moving but he grabs my hip.

"Sweetheart, stop. Please." I shake my head. "Abbie, please." He shudders as I ease up. "Good God, girl. You're sex mad."

I giggle. "Me?" I want to laugh at the thought, but then I think, yes, may be with Edward I could be. "I want to do it again, please."

He rolls his eyes. "Really?" he says, shocked.

"Really."

"Hell, give me five minutes!"

"I'll give you three!"

"You're insatiable, lady. Where's my blushing Abigail?"

"Mmm, that I am, Scott. And you now have two minutes left."

He laughs so loud he makes me jump.

"Really bossy all of a sudden, aren't we?"

I nod, poking my tongue out.

He flips me on to my back suddenly, and I scream. Then we both laugh. I laugh until my belly aches. And I feel that if he wasn't holding me down I'd float right off through the door on a cloud, because that's how he makes me feel, like I'm the most important thing in the world to him, and I know I'm going to love him for the rest of my life.

His finger traces my cheek and his smile melts my heart. His kiss is tender as we make love again.

Edward's sitting up against the headboard and I'm still astride him. My arms are still draped around his neck and my head is buried into the side of it. I keep kissing him teasingly. I think it's tickling him because every now and again he shudders. His arms hold me carefully as he kisses the side of my head.

I'm still trying to get my head back out of the clouds and come back down to earth.

Edward kissed every bruise and mark on my body. He made me cry twice, because although he never said as much I knew he was kissing me better; those weren't tears of sadness, but of love and happiness. I think he was baffled by my crying, and no doubt he'll ask me when he gets his breath back. I'm just going to be honest with him. I love him so much that I'm not going to let anything stand in our way or my happiness.

I'm taken aback by how determined and strong I am. This Adonis of a man underneath me has blown me out of the water. I'm not the same Abigail I was a few months ago. I'm happy, so happy. Though let's face it, who wouldn't be, straddling Edward Scott. I look at him. He smiles, and that smile is for me. It lights up the room, his face, and my heart.

He doesn't have to say anything to me – his eyes do all the work. I see love, happiness and desire in them, and it's all for me.

I sigh with satisfaction.

"Happy, contented, Abbie? Now you've had your wicked way with me again?"

I nod laying on his chest.

"Always, Edward."

He kisses me gently. "Are we sleeping like this?" he whispers.

"Yes," I say, yawning.

He moves forward and pulls the duvet over us both.

"No complaints from me, sweetheart. You can sleep on me anytime."

"Thank you. I think I will." I kiss him softly on his chest.

He holds me in his arms and we both fall fast asleep together, cocooned in our duvet, as one.

Chapter 6

I wake feeling really warm, that there's pressure on my body again, and my first thought is that the infection has come back. But then I realise it's Edward's strong arm draped around my waist, and the heat from his muscular body spooning me. I smile as my thoughts drift back to last night. I stretch out my arms and yawn, disturbing him slightly as he tightens his arm around me.

"Hmm, good morning, Abbie," he says sleepily.

"Good morning, Edward."

There's a brief silence as I feel his other hand cup my breast. My back is still to him and I grin, knowing exactly where this greeting is going. I cough slightly and he stops.

"Do you always greet your patients like this?" I whisper, feeling his erection firmly in the small of my back.

"Hmm …" He tugs at my erect nipples while thrusting harder into my back. "No, just you, Abbie." His voice is deep and muffled as he nibbles the back of my neck, making me squirm in his arms and sending shivers rippling down my spine. I catch my breath as his hand glides from my breast to my sex. I move slightly away from his hand, a little tender from last night.

"What's wrong?" he asks placing his hand on my tummy.

"I'm okay. Just a little sore."

"Where?" he asks in the same gravel voice, running his hand towards my sex again.

I roll my eyes and turn to face him. He knows exactly where.

"Did I work you too hard?" he says, with the sexiest smile planted on his face

I shake my head, and feel a flush creeping up my neck and onto my face, thought I can't fathom why.

"Oh, you're blushing now. I don't remember you blushing last night. I distinctly remember you asking me … to fuck you and fuck you hard."

My eyes close in response to his bluntness. I can feel my face getting hotter and it's frustrating because I did say that and I didn't want him to stop. So why am I flushed?

He laughs, knowing the effect he's having on me.

"Stop teasing, Edward."

He pouts. "Have you gone all shy on me?"

I raise my hand to slap him gently on his chest, but he's quick and grabs my hand. "Tut, tut, tut," he says firmly, and his eyes grow dark and mischievous. "I've a cure for shyness, Abbie." And he plants a kiss on my lips.

"Oh, you have, have you? And what might that be?" I reply, trying my best to sound matter of fact. "I'll show you," he almost shouts, kneeling over me, flipping me onto my back and pinning me down with my arms above my head. I squeal in shock.

"Oh, dear, are you not sensitive in the mornings?" he adds, and glides his tongue slowly over my breasts. "Must I stop?" he whispers, lifting his eyes to mine. I shake my head. "Good," he says firmly, "because I wasn't going to." As he continues rolling his tongue, tasting me, teasing me with the most delectable voice I've ever heard. I squirm underneath him. "Mmm … I've cured the shyness." He stares at me with that sultry look, waiting for me to answer. I nod. "So now to cure the soreness, Abbie." His voice is so inviting that I can't do anything but agree as he lowers his head.

I'm exhausted. I lie on my back, watching him move from the bottom of the bed. He stands, gloriously naked, and winks.

"Better."

I nod, smile, and stare at him. He has a satisfied grin planted on his face.

"You're staring, Abbie."

I poke my tongue out, then reply sleepily, "Yes, I seem to be, don't I? But was this your game plan all along, Edward?"

His expression is one of puzzlement. I think he's wondering what I'm going to say.

I clear my throat and speak, my tone serious. "I mean, enticing me back to your house, just so you can have your wicked way with me, morning, noon and night?"

He shrugs, clicking his fingers. He looks amused.

"You're on to me, aren't you?" I nod. "Another round?" I shake my head, thinking, *Just how much stamina does he have?* He winks again, grins, then huffs as though disappointed. "Well, I'll leave you to sleep then. We can skip noon if you're too tired." I raise my eyes, and he chuckles. "I'm sure I can wait until tonight."

I pull the duvet over my head. He is the bronze stallion on the mantle downstairs, and I wonder what on earth I've got myself into. He shouts as though the duvet is a thick door and I can't hear him underneath it. It's a bit like the magic curtains that surround a hospital bed. "I'm going for a shower; I'll see you downstairs when you've got your breath back."

I hear a door open, and him laughing at his own joke. I sigh, feeling happy at the sound. Then I close my eyes and fall fast asleep.

I stretch, and yawn. I'm aching and a little sore still. I blink my eyes, taking in the low sun that's steaming through the window. I smile as I inhale, catching a fresh breeze coming through the small opening in the window to the front of the house. I'm alone and naked in Edward's bed, and I wonder whether it's his intention to keep me this way. I grin, let out another big yawn, and think, *Well, there are worse things, I suppose.*

I see my bags on the floor next to the dressing table. I get up and amble over to them. I take out my toiletry bag and lay clean underwear and clothes onto the bed. Then I make my way to what I presume is the en-suite bathroom.

I enter. The lights come on automatically. There's a large dressing area. A brown leather chair sits in the middle of the room facing a large tilt-and-turn mirror. All around are rails and rails of designer suits, trousers and shirts. Tailored clothes, casual clothes, racks of shoes, boots, trainers – it's like a Mayfair tailor's. There's another sitting area with a mirror and a stool. I notice a bottle of his aftershave. I remove the lid and spray it into the room, inhaling the scent. It's Edward – fresh, masculine, alluring.

"Mmm …" I say under my breath. I close my eyes and his face appears in my mind.

"You like the smell of that, Abbie?" he asks curiously.

He startles me and I nearly jump out of my skin and drop the bottle on the floor.

"Bloody hell, Edward. Don't do that! Creeping up on me like that!" I'm more than a little embarrassed that he's caught me snooping.

He stands there with his head cocked to one side, then pushes open another door. The light floods in.

"Were you looking for the bathroom by any chance?"

I nod. He bows slightly, moves his hand towards the open door, and grins. "Well, there you go." His eyes are wide, cocky, and all over my naked body as I walk slowly past him. I stick up my nose as I reach him, like a naughty child who's just been caught with her hand in the cookie jar. Still, I can't resist a retort.

"You seem to be staring, Edward."

He slaps my bum as I walk into the bathroom.

"Ouch!" I shout and he smirks.

"Then put some clothes on." A silly noise leaves my throat – the cheek of him – and I'm just about to say something back when he says, "Shower, and then downstairs. I've started breakfast."

He closes the door behind him and I hear him laughing as he leaves the bedroom. Oh, Lord, he's doing that thing to me again, flustering me to the point where I get tongue-tied and can't answer.

The size and splendour of the bathroom take my breath away. There's a walk-in shower with two seats inside that facing each. It's enormous and looks extremely hi-tech. There's a beautiful roll-top bath, again for two, plus two sinks in tall cream-coloured cabinets. Everything appears to be for two … apart from the toilet. The walls are painted floor to ceiling in a plum colour of such high gloss that the effect is like glass. A large heated rail stands next to the shower draped with large plump towels.

I enter, slowly at first, as the floor is like the walls and appears slippery, though it turns out not to be.

I use the toilet and then go to flush but there's no handle or chain that I can see. There's a button on the wall just a metre or so above. I press it but nothing happens. I wave my hand over the button and the toilet flushes.

"Of course he'd have a hi-tech toilet," I say aloud as I make my way over to the shower.

The shower's all black and chrome inside. I close the door and the lights come on. I study the images on the control panel – Bluetooth, USB, telephone answering, radio, mood lighting, massage.

I press the massage symbol and I'm confronted with more pictures – a gentle trickle, full-body massage, or overhead rain shower from the ceiling. I look upwards and see holes in the top. It's like something from a sci-fi film. I press the symbol for full-body massage, thinking it'll help with my aches and pains. I wait a moment for it to start then scream in shock as freezing-cold water blasts me from about fifteen different jets. I shout and curse, then scramble to the control panel as I'm pelted in the face. I quickly press off and it stops.

My teeth chatter and my body's battered from the water. I look at the panel again, and press rain shower, this time waiting for it to start and hoping it's not a monsoon. Warm water sprays from above and I begin to relax as it gently cascades over my body. I take the shampoo and massage into my hair, then rinse and apply the conditioner.

I reach for Edward's shower gel from the glass shelf and apply a generous amount onto my hands then glide it over my skin, inhaling the fresh scent of lemons. I smile, thinking about my dream, and Edward's face appears in my mind. I'm getting that warm feeling inside again thinking about him as I rinse my hair and turn off the shower.

I step out onto the mat, grab one of the warm towels from the rail, and wrap it around me. I make my way to the sink, open my toiletry bag and take out my toothpaste. As I rummage for my toothbrush I hear a rustle beneath my finger. I immediately get a warm flush of anxiety. I screw up my face and look down at the missed doses.

"Shit." I put my hands to my face. "Shit." I panic as realisation sets in thick and fast. I start to ramble. "I can't be. Could I? Shit, Abbie, how stupid."

But I didn't think. But I was sick before going to the lakes and when I was there. I don't know if my pill would have still worked or not. But why, why didn't I think? Edward is going to be so cross with me. I need to do a test, and quick. I need to ring Alison, ask her to get me one to ask her if she's knows. I've no phone. Damn. I'll have to use Edward's.

I feel dizzy and scared, and my tummy churns. What if I'm pregnant? What's he going to say? What will he think? That I've done it to trap him? What if he doesn't want me? I take a deep breath, return to the bedroom and dress quickly, the what-ifs swimming in my head.

At the bottom of the stairs I'm met by Shadow and Edward.

"Hi." He holds out his hand gesturing with his head down the hallway. "It's this way."

I take his hand nervously and he smiles. Is he going to hate me?

"Abbie, your hand's shaking. What's the matter?"

I don't know what to say. I just stare, remembering what we promised each other. No secrets. But is this a secret? Because I don't know yet if I'm pregnant. But is it any wonder I forgot to take the bloody thing or even contemplated if it was working after vomiting, after everything that's happened. But I do feel like I'm deceiving him by not telling him, so should I just tell him?

"Tell me," he continues, as though he's read my mind. I suddenly feel confused. I try to pull my hand away. I want to run back up the stairs and hide.

I pull in a deep breath and bottle it. "Please can I borrow your phone?"

"Yes, but why?"

I can't tell him. I'm too scared of what his reaction will be.

"Please, Edward, just lend me your phone."

"Like I said, Abbie, no problem. But can't you tell me why?"

I shake my head, wanting to scream. All I need is to talk to Alison.

"Okay," he says, sounding disappointed.

He reaches into his pocket and passes me his phone. I snatch it from him which I don't mean to do, but I'm nervous, he raises his eyes in surprise.

"I'll leave you to make your call in private," he says. His voice sounds flat, offended. He turns and Shadow follows him along the hallway and through the door at the bottom. It closes with a slight bang.

I stare at the door, wondering if I've done the right thing. After all, this is about us, and though I'm not sure it'll matter to him, it does matter to me, but it does concern us both, whatever the outcome is.

I hold my breath, press the on-button and swipe the screen. I freeze and my heart misses a beat as I see his screen-saver. It's me, and I'm smiling and laughing. I notice it's The Drake, our first date. I'd no idea he'd taken a picture of me. I look so happy, young and full of life, and I know immediately not telling him first is wrong. My fear has made me offend him, yet I know he's nothing like Adam. He's wonderful and makes me happy.

I turn the phone off. I have to speak to Edward first, not Alison. I walk down the hallway and through the door. He turns as I enter. I expect a frosty reception as I hand him his phone, but I don't get one. I get a smile and an apology, and both these things give me the courage to trust him.

"I've not used your phone, but I do need to talk to you," I say. My voice shakes. His looks puzzled, but nods.

"I'm really sorry, Edward, but you see, I've not …"

"What is it, Abbie?"

"I've not been taking my pill, well I have but I …" His face freezes as I continue to babble. "I'm sorry – I forgot, well sort of forgot – but I was ill and in hospital." His eyes close. "I'm sorry, I didn't do it on purpose, honestly … Say something, Edward. Please."

He opens his eyes slowly and looks at me blankly.

"Were you ringing Alison?"

I nod.

"So why didn't you?"

"Because I couldn't keep it from you. I felt like I was deceiving you, and I realised I needed to speak to you first. Are you cross?"

"Pregnant …"

He shakes his head, then breathes out again long and hard as I stare at him. He runs a hand through his hair and I know that sign – he's frustrated. He doesn't know what to say or do. My heart sinks as he stares at me, looking completely lost.

"Yes, I could be," I say softly.

He walks over to the cooker and switches it off. Then turns to me.

"Then we'd better go and find out, though I think it's a little early to know."

I hold my head down, knowing I don't mean *this time,* although that's a worry as well. "I mean from the first time," I say feebly.

"What? What do you mean, the first time?" It's his work voice – full of authority and dominance.

"The first time we made love."

"You said you were on the pill."

"I was ... I am."

"So—" He runs a hand through his hair.

"I was sick at home and then in the Lakes, and I'm worried that the pill hasn't worked."

He shakes his head.

Frustration rises in me. "Hey, this is not just my fault; it takes two to tango. And last night you didn't seem to care." He stares, and I think he's blaming me. "You *are* a doctor, Edward, aren't you? You should have thought about this too."

"So should you – you're meant to be training as a nurse!"

I put my hands to my face and push the tears back in. I wonder what he's thinking. I'm scared because I've always wanted to be a mother – the thought is never far from my mind – but I know I can't be pregnant at this moment in time. If Adam were to find out I'm carrying Edward's child …

"When is your period due?" I shrug. "You don't know. How can you not know something like that?"

It's as though he's mocking me.

"Last week, this week … you're meant to be the bloody doctor, Edward."

"Yes, I am a bloody doctor, but I'm not telepathic, Abbie."

"Really?" I bite back. "That's a pity because when you have unprotected sex, is there not a possibility they might get pregnant?" I answer sarcastically. I'm cross – he's making out that this is all my fault.

His face is solemn, his tone flat. "I've never had unprotected sex with anyone except you. I trusted your word."

"Oh, well, lucky me," I snap, turning my back on him as the tears well. "So, then, do you think I'm lying to you?"

His hand comes to my shoulder, turning me to face him; he sees the tears in my eyes.

"Don't, Abbie."

"But—"

"I'm sorry I sounded harsh, but I don't know how to react. I'm scared, but don't think for one minute this is just down to you, because it's not. I should've realised about your pill. And, yes, I should've used protection. But I lost myself in you, because with you, Abbie, I always do."

I screw my face up, as tears threaten again. I feel so mixed up and confused; it's not the thought of being pregnant but of it happening now.

"What's done is done, and if you are pregnant … we'll deal with it." He lifts my chin and looks into my eyes. And no further words are spoken as we both walk down the hallway, out through the front door and towards the car, wondering whether we're going to be parents so soon.

Chapter 7

We sit in the 4x4 on the drive, seatbelts on, engine running. My hands are shaking, and Edward's face is set in a stunned expression. He breathes silently but I can see his chest moving in and out. I look out of the window. The snow's falling lightly and covers the two swans by the door. I'm uncertain how I feel … how Edward feels. What did he mean by "deal with it"? I place my hand discreetly on my tummy and feel the tears well in my eyes. What if I am pregnant and he doesn't want it? I could never get rid of it, or take a pill. I'd do it alone, move far, far away and be a single mum. He squeezes my knee, bringing me out of my daydream.

"Are you nervous?" I turn to look at him. My silence answers his question. He squeezes a little harder. "Me too! I've never thought about being a father before."

At least now I know what he meant; he'd be there for us both. But that nice warm feeling is wiped from my mind as I think of Adam and his cruelty, because I have no doubt in my mind what he'd do. And although I'm desperate to have a baby, and more so Edward's baby, I'm hoping I'm not pregnant – not until I can rid myself of Adam once and for all. I'm not sure if I can explain this to Edward, so I keep these thoughts to myself until I know what's going on.

We drive to the chemist on the high street. Edward buys the test, returns to the car and hands the paper bag to me. We drive home in a daze, both of us silent. I hold this little package in my hand, knowing it has our future inside, and wondering what that future will be.

We taking off our coats and boots in the hallway. I breathe in – the sound's louder than I'd intended. Edward's eyes meet mine.

"Come on. Let's just do it." He takes my shaking hand, leading me past the staircase and through a door into a cloakroom. "Do you know what to do, or do we have to read the instructions?"

"It's okay. I know how this goes."

"Do you want me to stay?" I shrug, not knowing what I what anymore. I fumble with the crumpled paper bag and it rustles in my shaking hands.

"I'm so scared, Edward," I whisper.

"It's okay. I am too. Let's do it together, then."

And I remove the box from the crumpled bag, open it and take the test from the foil packet.

I've done the test and we both stare at the little window in silence, wondering what the result will be. It's counting down slowly, bar by bar. I shut my eyes; I can't look. The test is on its final countdown. In one minute, this little plastic blue-and-white paddle with its plastic window and my pee on the tip, will determine our destiny.

It feels like an eternity, not three minutes. I turn quickly to Edward, who's looking at the test intently.

I bury my head into his chest, mumbling, "I can't watch."

He strokes the back of my head gently. "It's okay, Abbie. We'll know in a minute." He breathes in sharply.

"Has it finished? What does it say?"

He's silent for a second and strokes my hair again.

"It's finished," he says. His voice is flat.

I daren't look. I inhale, hold my breath, and turn my gaze to the test.

Not pregnant.

"Oh, thank goodness," I say louder than I'd intended, and I'm stunned by my words, but knowing in my heart of hearts it's for the best. He moves back from me, bemused.

"You're not upset, Abbie?"

I shake my head. "I'm relieved," I say honestly. "Aren't you?" I ask, surprised.

He smiles lightly, nods, and pulls me to him. We both sigh with relief.

Then he floors me. "But that doesn't mean I'll not get you pregnant in the future, Abbie."

I squeeze him to me as tight as I possibly can, feeling his smile as the tears come.

"And there's nothing on this earth that I'd like more."

He hugs me tightly.

"Quite right too."

I think he's trying to lighten the mood with his usual overconfident tone, but I don't snip at him, not this time, because I know I've baffled him with my reaction.

"Yes, Edward … quite right too!" I place my lips to his, and feel his smile on them as he kisses me back. I feel as though my body could just melt into his.

"Come on – let's get some breakfast. You've not eaten properly for days."

"But I don't feel like eating."

He ignores me and leads me towards the door at the bottom of the hall. We enter and Shadow runs to Edward, tail wagging, then saunters over to me.

"Take a seat." He points to the island in the centre of the room. "What would you like to eat?"

"I'm really not hungry Edward, honestly. Just a coffee would be nice."

His eyebrows raise and I know that look. I'm going to be fed whether I like it or not.

"Okay, you win – anything you want will be fine," I say, rolling my eyes as he walks towards the cooker, takes out what I presume is our previous breakfast and throws it in the bin. Shadow looks disappointed.

"You know you can't have it, Shadow."

Shadow puts his head to one side as if he understands what Edward has just said. It makes me chuckle.

"He has a very delicate stomach – a lot of things disagree with him, don't they, boy?" He pats him on the head, and Shadow looks pleased as punch, wagging his tail.

They look so good together it makes me smile. Edward smiles back and continues talking in a silly voice that owners reserve for their pets. "You're very sensitive, aren't you, boy?" Shadow makes a noise like he's answering him; it makes me laugh even more. Edward turns his eyes to me. "He's just like his master, Abbie – sensitive." I raise my eyes at him, as if to say, *Really, Edward? You, sensitive?* He glares at me with his brows raised. "I'm making you breakfast, aren't I? Is that not showing a sensitive side?"

I nod because I suppose it is. "Well I suppose it's a start," I say, and smirk.

He shakes his head, and turns to the espresso machine. Shadow makes his way over to me as the machine splutters steaming coffee into a cup. Edward passes it to me.

"Thank you," I say. He nods and returns to the cooker.

"Um, poached or scrambled?" He flips a frying pan in his hand like a cocktail shaker.

"I don't mind."

"Not fussy then," he remarks, turning to a large cupboard, which turns out to be an enormous fridge. He sticks his head inside and removes a large dish full of eggs. "Fresh from the farm down the road."

"Can I help?"

"No, you sit tight and drink your coffee," he says bossily. "Watch your master at work."

"My master?"

He winks, his eyes hooded with that suggestive look, although I'm not sure what he means by it. "My master, Edward?" I ask again.

"Well, if you play your cards right, I could be," he says with that boyish grin that I somehow can't resist, and he knows it.

"Shut up, and make my eggs," I say with a laugh.

"Don't get used to this, Abbie, because when you're better you can wait on me hand and foot," he replies, nodding like it's a foregone conclusion.

"I don't think so, Edward Scott."

"We'll see."

He's so bloody cheeky. I drink my coffee, watch Edward cook my breakfast and take in the impressive kitchen.

It's very masculine, just like him, and modern – which is unexpected from the outside – with highly polished grey fitted units, and every gadget known to man. A water machine, ice machine, CD player, iPod docking station, built-in television, and a marvel of culinary delights.

"You like to cook?" I ask, breaking the silence.

"I enjoy dabbling," he says, walking over to the island setting the places for us. "Toast?" I nod and Edward places a plate in front of me.

"Thank you," I say, looking at my eggs, poached to perfection and sitting on a bed of hot buttered, wholemeal toast. I slice into one of the eggs and the most satisfying yellow yolk oozes onto my toast. "Mmm, tastes delicious. I didn't realise how hungry I was."

Edward nods and tucks in.

He finishes before me and waits for me to finish before clearing the plates.

"Would you like to talk about the test, Abbie, and what we plan to do about a further one?"

I finish my last mouthful and raise my eyes. I knew we'd have to address it at some point and I suppose it's better sooner than later.

"I was quite taken aback by your response. Being relieved, I mean. I sort of thought you'd be upset."

And I know he means because of my history with Adam.

"You do know I wasn't suggesting you get rid of the baby or take the morning-after pill."

I nod. "I know that, Edward. It's just … I suppose … I'm relieved because I don't think it's right at this moment in time – with everything that's happened and everything that's about to happen."

"About to happen?" he says, puzzled.

"Yes, like I said before, I'm going to the solicitor, and I'm going to file for a divorce. I know Adam's not pleased about that; he said so when he rang me."

"When he rang you?" His tone is sharp.

"Yes. I told you – when I was at the Lakes."

He nods, remembering. "What did he actually say?" His tone is reserved and I can tell he's not happy but trying his best to contain himself.

"I told you – he threatened me, said he'd worked too hard for it, by which I presume he meant my money. He wants what's his, or what he thinks is his. And, like you, I think it was all premeditated."

He looks at me, realising what I've just said, because we haven't had that conversation.

"Premeditated?"

I nod. Now he knows I was listening to the conversation with him and my gran in my hospital room.

"Sorry, yes. I heard everything. I know it was rude of me to pretend to be asleep, but I knew that you wouldn't have had that conversation if I was awake. And I needed to know what was happening."

"Yes, you did, and I was going to tell you, and about Simon."

"I know, but I also thought you might leave out some of the detail to protect me."

He shrugs, as if to confirm my suspicion.

"So you see, that's why I'm relieved I'm not pregnant, because I know how devious Adam is. And if he thought for one minute that I was pregnant with your child …" I shut my eyes not wanting to go down that road, but I need to tell him. So I open them looking straight at him and I'm about to speak but he answers for me.

"You thought he'd harm the baby like before," he says softly. I nod. "Then I fully understand, Abbie. But believe me, he'll not lay a finger on you ever again. I'll make sure of that."

"I know, Edward." I doubt he'd even let Adam breathe on me again.

"Do you want me to come to the solicitors with you?"

"No, thank you. I feel up to it now and I'd like to do this on my own. I hope you don't mind. But I need to start taking back my independence."

He reaches over and pats my hand.

"Yes, of course." Then he winks. "What would you like to do today?"

"I'd like that grand tour you promised me."

He gets up and starts to fill the dish washer. I don't feel sad or jittery at the thought of not being pregnant – well, not from the first test anyway – and for some reason I don't feel scared at the thought of going to the solicitor either. And that's because of Edward. I know that he's here, that we're together, and we're starting to build a life with each other as equals.

Then he turns, and I see the expression on his face – something has just dawned on him.

"You said a grand tour, Abbie?" I knew I wouldn't get a grand tour.

He shakes his head, and I hold my laugh inside because I know what he's going to say next.

"A whistle-stop tour, that's what you'll have." He waits for me to agree, then raises his eyebrows, like he's aghast by the thought of a grand tour. And in his work tone he continues, "You're still meant to be recuperating, remember?" As if, somehow, I'd forgotten.

I've no strength at the moment for a comeback, so I say, "Okay, a whistle-stop tour will do for now."

He thinks he's won that little battle. I smirk inside and let him think he has.

We've done the inside tour – if it had been any quicker, or I'd blinked, I'd have missed it. He did allow me to pop my head into the rooms, though.

The house is spectacular. Downstairs, there are five rooms, plus an office, the kitchen, a laundry, and the cellars. The sitting room is the most impressive I've seen in a long time – large but cosy and elegant with old wooden floorboards. Light flooded in through the two large windows. I instantly loved it even though I only popped my head in, but the feeling I got from the room was nice. There are seven bedrooms – five en suite – and two bathrooms.

Next, I walk the grounds with him, see the garage and the cars. His fourth car I'd not seen before, but, wow, the silver e-type Jag is amazing. He says he can't wait to take me out in it in summer. I nod eagerly like a child.

I meet three beautiful horses, though I'm scared of them. Edward tells me that he rides them, but puts them to stud too. They even have an equine passport, which I find amusing, and try my best not to laugh, imagining them going through passport control. The smile soon lifts from my face when he tells me the fee he charges – nearly one and a half thousand pounds for a mare to be covered by one of his stallions, a horsey term for the stallion having his wicked way with the mare.

Edward grins, saying he doesn't use the AI method. I ask what he means and he explains that mares are quite nasty to the stallions when they mate, so some use fake mares to collect sperm. I pull a face and tell him to stop. He laughs and comments, 'Yes, where's the fun in that?' I just raise my eyes, thinking, *Why would he think anything different?*

There are two chestnuts, both liver-coloured. One – Autumn Storm – has a white stripe down its face; Edward calls it a blaze. The other – Silent Mist – looks like he's wearing a white ankle sock on his front leg. Edward recounts an old tale his grandad told him when he was a little boy.

'Four white socks, keep him not a day. Three white socks, send him far away. Two white socks, give him to a friend. One white sock, keep him till the end.'

He says his grandad was a firm believer in old wives' tales. It used to be thought that pale hooves were weaker than black ones, and the more white socks a horse had, the paler its hooves, meaning it was weaker.

I just nod, feeling sorry for the socked horses, but knowing that Silent Mist is a keeper.

The black stallion shines like polished ebony. His mane glistens in the low sun and dances down his neck and on to his back. He reminds me of the gymnasts I used to watch as a child, performing their ribbon routines with such elegance. And of Edward, stunning and proud, and I say as much. He laughs, saying he's flattered indeed to be compared to such a fanatic specimen. And more so when I add that I wouldn't pay him one and a half thousand pounds to cover me. His reply is blunt. "I'd gladly pay one and a half thousand pounds to fuck you senseless in a barn or a field." I ignore his remark, which makes him laugh, more so when I say, "I preferred the horsey term – far more eloquent."

When he tells me the stallion's name – As Good As It Gets – I can't help but wonder if he thinks the same about me, but I don't say anything. I just hold in my fear and stroke each of the stallions in turn as we pass them. They seem to like it, and stay calm.

We leave the stable block and make our way down a path towards the back of the house. We pass large empty plots with nothing in them but soil.

"Vegetable plots," Edward says.

"You grow your own vegetables? Is there no end to your talents?" I say a little mockingly.

"I'm afraid the talents of the vegetable plots are again down to Jimmy." I'm surprised that there's no further comeback, but then he says, "Although you've only tasted a very small selection of my many talents, Abbie."

"I have?"

His eyes darken and they're so arousing that my pulse races. I consider the talents I've experienced so far.

"You're blushing, Abbie. I wonder what you're thinking about!"

"Do you think of nothing else?"

"No! And I can't wait to show you."

I roll my eyes in defeat, knowing that no matter what my comeback, he'll turn it into something sexual. He grins as he punches another code into a gate that leads to the grassed area I saw from the bedroom window. Shadow runs ahead, stopping a hundred metres or so in front of us, then turns to see if Edward is still there.

"Oh, can we walk to the lighthouse, Edward?"

"No, not today. It's further than you think."

"How far?"

"About a mile and a half."

"Gosh, it doesn't look that far. Is this where you come with Shadow? Where you told me you ran on the beach with him?"

"Yes. It's about five miles in total, and you have to be very careful with the tide. It's a creeper."

"What does that mean?"

"It comes in fast, and can surround you quickly, leaving you stranded. A lot of people drowned back in the day of pirates and smugglers. That was before the lighthouse was built, which is good for ships that are passing to port, but not so good for the stranded person on the beach. If the tides don't get you, the rocks that surround the lighthouse will surely end your days."

"Heck, I'll have to remember that."

"You must never come down here on your own," he says firmly, as if I'm a child. I just shrug. "I mean it! It's extremely dangerous, especially when you don't know the tides or the coastline," he snaps.

"Okay, I promise. I'll not come down here on my own."

"Good."

I take his hand and we walk a little further. I ask him to tell me the stories he knows about the pirates and smugglers. I listen, fascinated, and watch Shadow jumping in the tall grass and barking at the seagulls and the snow that's started to fall again.

Then the snowfall becomes heavier so we turn around and head back to the cottage.

We arrive back, entering through the front door and start removing our wet things before hanging them in the downstairs cloakroom.

"Hot drink?"

"Oh, please," I say, shivering.

Edward points to the sitting room and we go in. I sit on the sofa, watching him light the fire in the grate. When he's happy with it, he turns.

"I'll make you that drink now."

Shadow jumps up to follow him. He whispers something to him and to my surprise the dog walks towards me and sits at the side of my leg, but watches Edward walking out through the door. Leaving me and Shadow alone.

I wander from the sofa and look around. Shadow, true to his name, is right behind me. Above the fire is a large painting of a lone Stag. I glance at it, but don't linger as it brings back bad memories. I walk over to the window and look at the snow. I see the swans at the door. I smile, pat Shadow on the head, and walk back to the sofa. I yawn and Shadow cocks his head. I smile as it reminds me of Edward.

I sit down again and Shadow practically sits on my feet. I take in the room with its two large windows that flood the room with light. Lots of highly polished antique furniture is spread around the room. There are two large sofas either side of the fire in a soft chestnut brown. Chairs, formal and easy, are dotted around. The floor is of old wood, like in the hallway, highly polished and partially covered by an expensive-looking rug. I wiggle my toes in the deep soft pile and yawning again; the logs are throwing heat into the room, making it cosy.

Edward enters. "Are you tired, Abbie?" I nod as he places the drinks tray onto a little table next to the sofa, and grabs a throw from the back of a chair. "Here, put your feet up."

I lie back, feeling sleepy. He sits at the side of my feet and passes me my drink. "You can't beat hot chocolate, snow and a roaring fire," he says, smiling.

I taste my chocolate. "Wow, that's strong. What's in it?"

"Lashings of Baileys. Do you like it?"

"Yes, it delicious," I reply, licking the chocolate from my lips.

He taps my leg. "A film?"

I nod, as he picks up a remote and presses a button. Doors suddenly open to what I thought was an antique sideboard, revealing yet another top-of-the-range gadget – the largest television I've ever seen, and probably the most expensive. Sound engulfs the room, throwing music and voices around as if they're in the room with us. Shadow makes a noise like he's yawning, curling himself into a ball at Edward's feet in front of the roaring fire.

I turn to rest my head on Edward's shoulder then glance at the television. It's one of my favourite films. *Scrooge.*

I sigh contentedly as his arm goes around me. I snuggle into him, so much in love that I feel as if I'm in a film myself, the one where it's right at the very end, where she gets her happy ever after. And then it dawns on me – why I feel the way I do about it. I look round again, seeing the roaring fire, the rugs between the sofas, the hot chocolate and snow outside, and my heart flutters. Because it reminds me of home. Home with my gran and grandad when I was young. And these feelings I'm experiencing are of safety and love.

My eyes start to close and I begin to drift into what I know will be a wonderful dream.

Chapter 8

I sit at the island drinking my coffee, talking to Shadow, waiting for Edward to finish getting ready for work.

"I've missed our walk this morning, Shadow," I say, and he stares at me as if he understands what I'm saying. Edward and I have walked him to the lighthouse every morning except today, when Edward took him alone when he went for a run on the beach.

I smile warmly, knowing Edward is ready and leaving the bedroom. Shadow's told me; his head is cocked to one side as he hears Edward's footsteps upstairs. I pat him on the head although he doesn't move his gaze from the ceiling. His eyes are bright and astute. He lowers his head slightly as he follows Edward's movements on the stairs. Then he bounces forward, tail wagging, as Edward reaches the hallway. Shadow bounds out through the door to welcome him.

"Hello, boy. Where's Abbie?" Shadow has skidded to a halt and Edward pats him. Shadow barks and runs into the kitchen. Edward follows.

"Perfect timing," I answer, and remove his coffee from the espresso machine. "Do you have time for breakfast?"

"No, sweetheart, just this," he says, taking a large gulp of his coffee.

"How come I have to eat breakfast and you skip it?" I ask.

"Because you do!" He finishes his coffee. "And have you? Eaten breakfast?"

"Not yet. Why, Mr Bossy?"

He grins. "Just looking after you, dear."

I laugh as he gets his things together, then glance outside.

The snow's gone now, so Edward's driving the BMW to work, though I know the real reason – the weather forecast last night said it might snow later on today, so he's insisted I have the 4x4.

I have appointments today; I'm meeting my gran in town and we're going to the solicitor's. Then I have a doctor's appointment to ensure that my pill's working correctly and the infection has cleared. I feel it has but Edward insisted I got checked out again. I'm not panicking any more about the scare because I've had my period. But Edward wants me to have a urine test, just to be sure.

I lift my eyes, remembering the scare we had last week, and what happened the day after that. I came on my period and I think we both sighed a breath of relief, truth be told. Edward nagged me, then insisted I put the date on my calendar and set a reminder each day to take my pill. It irked me but I silently agreed after a couple of days because I couldn't put up with the constant badgering from him. Or the fact that he threated to do it himself. I had of course been going to do it, had thought it a good idea until he said "I had to take some responsibility". There were some other things said that got my back up, and I muttered defensively under my breath about it always being a woman's job to take all the precautions.

I was mad with him; told him he should really think about his words before letting them roll off his tongue. He laughed then, as always, and said the nicest things to me. And I felt guilty. Of course.

We've talked and talked about it and I found it very easy to explain my fears. He said he'd like a family with me one day, which brought tears to my eyes. He hugged me, saying I was sweet, and that I'd make a wonderful mother. I told him he'd make an amazing father, and he smiled a little nervously. We've been for walks, eaten together in the evening, watched telly curled up on the sofa in front of a roaring fire. And had lots of wonderful baths in the roll-top, where I experienced more of Edward's talents. My cheeks flush a little as I remember. We've made love a lot, unable at times to keep our hands off each other. And, honestly, every time was different, amazing. But the thing I've enjoyed most is how much we've laughed together – laughed until our bellies hurt. I love his company so much; it's as if I've known him all my life. He's become my lover, my best friend, my everything.

"What time are your appointments today, Abbie?" he says, bringing me out of my daydream. I turn to look at him and wonder whether he knows how much he's changing my life.

"Nine thirty at the solicitor's, and eleven at the doctor's."

He nods. "Keep your phone on. I'll ring you – I could've come with you, you know."

I know he would've come if I'd have asked, but he's respecting my need to do this on my own and gain some of my independence back. Gran asked if she could come, but I'm not sure why. I asked, but she kept changing the subject. I spoke with Edward about it, and he said it was probably so I didn't get tongue-tied or frustrated. I agreed, thinking no more about it, although I think deep down he's glad she's going with me. She must have a good reason as she never normally asks anything of me.

"What time did you say for the doctor's?"

I know what he's thinking.

"Eleven. Why?"

"Hopefully it'll be good news, and I can throw those bloody plastic bags away and just—" He blows out a big breath of air. I laugh. "Can't think of that now, or I'll be late for work." Then he plants a huge kiss on my lips. "Now listen," he says, now serious, "are you sure about driving the 4x4?"

"Yes. Hell, you've given me enough test drives."

"Better to be safe than sorry. Do you remember the codes for the gates? And have you got your urine sample?"

"Yes," I say, getting slightly annoyed.

"Just making sure."

I roll my eyes as he plants another delicious, lingering kiss on my lips, and I growl at him. He taps my bum, then squeezes it firmly. "Mmm … you're going to make me late for work again, Abbie."

"I'm not the one doling out bum squeezes and kisses."

"I know, but I can't resist you."

I laugh. "What time are you home tonight?"

"About five," he says, running a finger down the side of my face.

"Shall I make us dinner?"

"Now that's what I like to hear – my woman at home in my kitchen, making me dinner. Although I might call home at noon for lunch, now!" There's a dark gleam in his eye that makes me tingle.

"Off to work, you Neanderthal."

He laughs loudly and Shadow barks. Then he walks down the hallway towards the front door with the dog hot on his heels. He stops and bends, whispering something into Shadow's ear. Shadow runs down the hallway towards me and presses himself close to my leg.

"Edward, what have you just said to Shadow?"

"Nothing!" he shouts. "See you tonight." And he closes the door behind him.

I stand puzzled for a moment and pat the dog.

"Come on, boy. It's just you and me now," I say.

We go to the kitchen, and I tidy up. Then I put on a washer-load of whites –mainly Edward's shirts and a few of my things. Edward told me not to do any of this as he has a housekeeper who comes four times a week, but I shook my head saying it was the least I could do, and that I didn't like the idea of someone else washing my underwear. I laughed when he told me I knew his housekeeper – Yvonne from the hospital, which made sense when I pondered on the thought. She'd said a few things in the past, and at the time I thought they were a little strange – how she knew about Edward, and how he appeared at the strangest of times. He roared when I said he had spies everywhere.

I make my way to the cloakroom off the hallway, slightly tucked under the centre staircase, the one I did the test in last week. It's a bit like mine at home, except it doesn't lead to the cellar, which at Edward's is accessed via the laundry room. There's a toilet and wash basin, pegs to hang coats, and a shoe rack. I grab my coat and pull on my boots, then nearly fall backwards over Shadow.

"What's the matter, boy? Are you missing Edward too?" He doesn't answer, of course, but does that thing with his head.

I walk into the hall and make my way to the front door. I stop at the little dish on the sill of the window illustrating the church. I stare at the glass and twizzle my hand in the dish for the car keys to the Range Rover. I giggle as I notice a sticker on the key-fob with the code to the gates; there are two more keys with stickers on that read front door and back door.

"God, he thinks he's so bloody funny," I say to Shadow as I nearly fall over him again. "I'm going now; you go to bed." But he sits firm, looking at me. "Shadow, go to bed," I repeat, raising my voice, but he doesn't move. "Oh, please yourself," I say, and turn the key in the lock. He barks as the door opens. "Stop that, Shadow. What's the matter?" His head goes to one side, as I glance at my watch. "Come on. I'll be back soon." If I don't leave now I'll be late.

I walk out through the door. Shadow barks, which is unusual; he just usually trots off to his bed when Edward leaves. I can hear him behind the door; he seems to be whimpering. I should go back into him but I'm going to be late and I'll hit all the traffic if I leave it much longer.

I sit in the 4x4, deliberating whether to go back in for the dog. What if he's ill? I glance at the clock on the dashboard. Eight fifteen. I shake my head, start up the engine and drive down to the gates. I chuckle with satisfaction as I enter the code in the keypad, not once looking at the sticker. I turn the radio on and wait for the gates to open. The presenter is telling the listeners there are only seven days left until Christmas. I smile, wondering what this year will be like. Edward is so organised. We've been invited to his parents' house for Christmas; all his family goes – his brother, and two sisters and their children. I was a little torn, and told him I really wanted to spend it with him, but wanted to be with my gran too. So he made a phone call then took me by surprise – he'd go with me to my gran's for Christmas Day if I'd go with him to his parents' for Boxing Day. I nodded, knowing he was just perfect. Gran was thrilled when I called her.

I drive down the unmade road and turn left into Portland Drive. Gosh, it's a dream to drive and I feel so high up. I could well get used to this car, although I have my eye on the Aston. I told Edward this, but he said, "Hands off – that's mine." "We'll see," I replied, and I winked. He grinned, knowing exactly what I was doing – "That won't work either, missy!"

I sing along to all the Christmas songs playing on the radio; they're really getting me in the spirit. I arrive on the high street in time for my appointment despite the heavy traffic. I drive to the car park at the back of the deli that's reserved for staff and deliveries, and take a space I know will be empty – my gran's.

There are two men in the unloading bay. One of them shouts, "Hey, love, you can't park there."

"Really, Ted?"

"Hell, sorry, Abbie. New wheels. Didn't recognise you there for a minute."

"They belong to a friend."

"Must be a good friend, letting you drive that. They cost a bloody bomb."

I smile. "Has my gran arrived yet?"

"I don't think so. I've not heard or seen her as yet."

"Okay. I'll go inside and wait. It's a little cold out here."

"Get one of the girls to make you a coffee."

"Don't be daft. I can make my own. Would you both like one?" I ask Ted and the driver. They both say yes and tell me their sugar requirements.

I walk past them and into the deli's busy seating area. I'm making my way around the counter when I'm stopped by an assertive young girl.

"I'm sorry, miss," she says firmly but politely. "You can't come around here. It's for staff only."

I smile. "It's Okay, I'm Abigail, Mrs Baxter's granddaughter." I say as Ted walks in.

"Everything all right, Abbie?"

"Yes, fine, thank you." I answer Ted, before smiling at Marie.

I turn towards the door that's just opened, letting in a cold breeze. I hear a loud voice that makes me smile.

"Abigail, sorry I'm late, dear," Gran says, rushing in and glancing at the clock before kissing me on the forehead. "Gosh, it's freezing. I think it might snow later. Some cheeky devil has parked in my space and William had to drop me at the front. Honestly, those 4x4 drivers think they own the roads *and* private parking spots. I bet most of them can't even read."

I pull a daft face. Gran looks puzzled.

"Sorry, it was me, Gran."

"You mean to tell me that you've finally bought a decent car?"

I can see the shock in her eyes.

"Not quite. It's Edward's."

She smiles warmly. "And how is he?"

"He's fine."

"I thought he might have wanted to come today."

"Hmm," I say and raise my eyes.

"You wanted to do it alone?" I nod. "Are we ready then?"

"Yes," I say, and thread my arm through hers.

She smiles as we walk out through the door and into the cold December morning towards the solicitor's.

"Have you time for lunch today?"

"No, not today. I've a doctor's appointment after the solicitor's." She looks a little worried. "I'm okay – it's just a check-up," I say quickly. She lifts her head. "And I want to pick a present up for Edward."

"Have you thought of what to get him?"

"I have an idea. I'm going to have a look in Forbes before my doctor's appointment."

"Really?" She smiles. "It must be serious."

I know what I want to buy him for Christmas. I ponder the thought as we continue up the high street. Then I think about Gran, and what to buy her, Glenda and William. There's also Alison and Tom, and Edward's parents – do I get them something? I look at Gran, then nod.

"Abbie, are you okay?"

"Yes, but I've just had a thought."

"We're going to Edward's parents on Boxing Day."

"Yes."

"I've not met them; do I take them a present?"

"No, Abbie. Take a gift instead, a kind of thank you for inviting you."

"Oh, yes, but what?"

"What about one of the deli's Christmas hampers?"

"Brilliant idea, Gran." She beams. "I'm paying for it though, or I'll not take it."

"Okay. When we're done at the solicitor's I'll ask Ted to make one up. Which one do you want?"

"A medium one – in a basket."

She smiles. "Nice choice. And price?"

"A hundred. Will that be okay?"

"Yes, that'll be fine." I go into my handbag.

"Abbie," she says.

I ignore her and give her the money for the hamper. "If you don't put it in your bag then I'm not having the hamper, because it would be a gift from you and not me."

"You're like your father in so many ways, Abbie."

I nod firmly and make sure she takes the money. "I'm glad I am."

I open the door to the solicitor's and we step inside.

Chapter 9

We sit in the reception area, waiting for Mrs Bradshaw. She enters through a doorway and greets us. She appears friendly and confident as she shakes our hands in turn. Her voice is pleasant, with no accent.

"Mrs Daxter, Abigail, so nice to see you. Please come this way." She gestures for us to follow her through to her office. We walk in and take a seat in front of her desk. The office is warm and light. A book case bursting with legal tomes takes up one side of the office, and framed certificates cover another wall. The room smells of polish and old leather. I study her, wondering how old she may be – late thirties, early forties maybe. She's not pretty, exactly, but attractively smart. Her hair's cut into an immaculate blonde bob, which suits her face. She's not slim, but not fat either. I'd say pleasantly round, but again, it suits her. She's dressed in a very nice tailored black skirt suit, high heels, and a light-blue blouse. Her makeup is understated, which makes her look trustworthy. On first impressions, I like her.

There's a brown paper file with my name on a tag at the side. Her computer is to the side, with two photo frames positioned so I can't see who's in them.

Gran breathes in; she seems a little uneasy, and I look at her as Mrs Bradshaw opens the file and speaks.

"Abigail, is the situation still the same as when we spoke on the phone?" I nod. "So you're filing for a divorce on the grounds of infidelity. Is that correct?"

"Yes, Mrs Bradshaw, everything's the same. I want a divorce on those grounds."

"And do you still think that Adam will contest it?"

I shrug. "I don't know what he'll do, but I know he'll want half the money from the sale of the house."

She looks back and forth between me and Gran.

"Abigail," my gran says, "I need to tell you something about the house. That's why I asked if I could come here with you today."

"What's the matter? What do you need to tell me?"

"Adam won't get any money from the sale of the house."

I look at her, shocked.

"Of course he will. We're married so he's entitled to half."

"That would be true if the house were in your name."

"Gran, what are you saying? You know the house belongs to me."

She doesn't answer, but stares back at me.

"Mrs Baxter, may I please explain to Abigail about the house?" says Mrs Bradshaw.

Gran nods and I look at them both in turn, somewhat confused.

"Abigail, when you were a little girl, when your parents died in the car crash, everything they owned was left to you, as was stipulated in their will. And you being the only child were the sole beneficiary of their estate." I nod; I already know this. "The will covered what would happen in the event of their deaths should you not be of age. They stipulated that the monies from the estate were to be held in trust by your grandparents."

"When I was twenty-one, although I never took it."

I look at Gran.

"I need to be clear, Abigail, as to why you never took it."

"Because I didn't want the money. Gran and Grandad made the appointment at the solicitor's – this one in fact – a few days after my twenty-first birthday. They both sat me down and spoke to me, told me they'd arranged the meeting, but I refused to go. In fact, it was me who cancelled the appointment."

"May I ask why?"

"Because I didn't want their money – I wanted them."

She nods at my gran, and I'm now confused as to what this all means.

"So who do you think has charge of your money now?"

I shrug. "I don't know. Me, I presume."

She shakes her head.

"I thought it automatically went to me."

"No, Abigail, it didn't. You needed to sign legal papers along with me and your grandad for that to happen," Gran says quietly.

I raise my eyes. "But I never signed any papers."

"I know. So do you understand what that means, Abigail?" she says.

"No, no I don't, Gran. What do you mean?"

"It means the monies and the house are still in your gran's name, as your grandad's passed away," Mrs Bradshaw says.

My eyes go wide.

"Abigail, I'm sorry, but you were so upset after your birthday that we found it very hard to speak to you about the money. Then Grandad passed away not long after."

I squeeze her hand. "I know," I say. It upsets me to see my gran like this; she looks apprehensive, which isn't like her. She's always in control of everything. She squeezes my hand back.

"And then you married Adam, and I tried so hard to speak to you about the money. And your grandad had asked me to take care of you—"

"God, stop this, Gran. You've always taken care of me!"

"Not just that way, but financially as well. But I saw what Adam and his mother were like about money." She breathes out as though she's struggling to explain. "And I know you bought the car he drove."

"You did. How?"

She breathes in even deeper. "I knew from your allowance that you weren't spending the money on yourself."

"I don't understand. Allowance? Where did that come from?"

"From me, Abigail."

"Why from you?"

"Because – I wanted to make sure you had things you needed."

"I had my job."

"I know you did, but I still put money in to your account every month."

I'm staring at her, puzzled. "I had no idea. I got my wage each month, and never spent more than I earned. And, yes, I saved some, which I used to pay for the car that Adam drove."

She nods again as if she knew. "Did you never check the statements?" Mrs Bradshaw asks.

I shake my head.

"What did you do with them?" I shrug again, feeling bloody stupid.

"I never got one. Adam always did the banking online, said it was safer and easier that way. You must both think I'm an idiot."

"No. Honestly, Abigail, there are names for men like him who prey on vulnerable women. Who manipulate, control them. I think Adam is narcissistic."

"What on earth does that mean?"

"Their behaviour is characterised by exaggerated feelings of self-importance, a need for admiration, and a lack of understanding of others' feelings."

I listen to Mrs Bradshaw's speech; it sounds rehearsed.

"A mental disorder?" Gran asks loudly. "Are you saying he's ill?"

"Something like that. It makes a lot of sense from what he's done and what Abigail's told me."

I glare at Mrs Bradshaw to stop her from talking. She knows everything that's happened, but Gran doesn't, and I want it to stay that way.

"But of course," she says quickly, "that's not for me to decide. I'm not a doctor. I was merely offering my opinion, and I'm sure he'd never agree to a test. So let's just forget I mentioned it."

I knew I should have come on my own. Gran stares at Mrs Bradshaw and I'm convinced she knows more than I've told her, but she doesn't say anything. But now I can't stop thinking about what Mrs Bradshaw has said. It does sort of make sense, though it's no excuse. I sit up in my chair and break the silence.

"I think, Mrs Bradshaw, we can all agree that he's sick," I say flatly. "And now preying on another woman."

I didn't want to bring Nicky into the conversation, but Gran knows about her and I need her to focus on today's agenda. There's another brief silence as they seem to digest my words. But I sit and wait, leaving the floor open for Mrs Bradshaw.

"Yes. I think we can agree on that, Abigail," she says, and Gran nods. "Did you not know that your gran was putting money into your current account?" I think she's trying to change gran's train of thought.

"No. Like I said, I'd no idea, and it's pretty obvious that Adam knew I didn't know, because he knew I'd give it back." She nods. "He'd also know my gran would never ask me about the money she was putting into the account, so that left him to do as he pleased with it."

"Have you any idea what money was going into your current account each month?"

"How could I if I never knew it existed?"

"What about the yearly one?"

"No," I reply firmly. I feel annoyed.

"I'm sorry, but I do need to ask these questions."

I nod. I'm not cross with her or my gran, but with Adam, and how I've been played all these years. I don't know if he's taken money out of my account, or spent any of the money Gran was putting into it, but I need and want to find out.

"Can you tell me, Gran, how much money you put into my account each month and how much went into my yearly account?" I ask, utterly drained, but seething inside.

She nods and squeezes my hand. "I put two thousand pounds in each month … and twenty-five thousand annually."

I put my head in my hands. I'd known about the annual account, but had no idea when it started or how much went into it.

"So the yearly account started when I was twenty-one?"

Gran shakes her head. "No. When you were five."

I swallow hard, knowing I'm going to cry, because that's just months after my parents died. Gran squeezes my hand even tighter.

"I'm sorry, sweetheart, but that was another stipulation from the will. And we tried to talk to you about it, but the mere mention of money from your parents sent you into silence."

I nod. "Was that also in trust?" I ask.

Gran shakes her head wearily, and stares at Mrs Bradshaw.

"No, that was in an account for you to spend on anything you wanted."

"So Adam had access to that account as well?"

"Only if you signed papers to give him access. Did you?"

I'm trying to think.

"I don't think so, just papers for the joint—"

I looking at them both, bite my lip and close my eyes. I did sign papers. I never read them, just signed my name. They could've been for anything. God, I've been so bloody gullible. All this that's happened, what he's done, he's done for money.

"Why, Gran? Why did they have to die? It's not fair. All this wouldn't be happening if they'd lived, or if I'd died with them."

"Stop that right now, Abigail. Don't you ever, ever, say that again, do you hear me?"

I'm shocked because she's never spoken to me like that before. And this is what I need to be told, because this could have been so dangerous for me, this could have sent me back. I pull in my stomach and sit up straight.

"Yes, you're right, Gran. It's just the thought ..."

"I know – so let's deal with him." She smiles, then addresses Mrs Bradshaw. "Mrs Bradshaw, do we have a plan?" she asks assertively. And this is my corporate gran speaking now. "Abigail, are we going to fight Adam and get you that divorce?"

She nods her head sharply towards me.

"Yes. Yes, we are!" I say, sitting up straighter in my chair and feeling a buzz of adrenaline.

"Mrs Bradshaw, do you want to explain or shall I?"

Mrs Bradshaw shrugs. "It's up to you."

"Then please begin. After all, this is what we're paying you for."

The solicitor clears her throat before speaking. "So, Abigail, the house … Since it's in your gran's name, Adam cannot take half the value of it, as legally it doesn't belong to you." I nod, processing what's being said. "And the money that's in trust to you is still under the guardianship of your gran. Which, if these figures are up to date, is a sizeable fortune, standing at one point three million pounds."

"What?" I shout, sitting bolt upright in my chair. "N-No, I've heard you wrong. Did you say …" Mrs Bradshaw nods. "Bloody hell." I breath in deep, trying to comprehend the amount. Then a shudder runs over me as if someone has walked on my grave. "Would he have known?"

"May be not the total, Abigail, but a rough estimate." She smiles sympathetically towards me and my gran. "The size of your parents' estate when they died was common knowledge."

I remember the attention their deaths drew in the tabloids. I'd heard a conversation about it between my gran and grandad. When I turned twenty-one, a local reporter printed something in the paper about my coming of age and being an heiress to the Baxter fortune. I also overheard Grandad on the telephone, blasting the newspaper. And while a few people in the village knew who I was, not many others did because I never advertised the fact that I was that Baxter.

But now everything seems to be slotting into place. God, why on earth did I not see it coming? Premeditated. Edward was right, premeditated down to the fine details and with a capital P. I feel ashamed and disgusted.

"Abigail, you need to do something for me."

I nod. I'll do whatever she tells me to.

"I want you to go to the bank and open a new account. Transfer the money from your joint current account with Adam, and any others he has access to. Then close those accounts. Don't worry about the trust accounts – he can't access those unless your gran signed the papers. Which we know she's never done."

Gran nods in agreement.

"Is it worth changing the accounts? I'm damned sure there will be nothing in them, and I can't do a thing about that, can I?"

"Unfortunately not, but you do need to remain positive, Abigail. He can't take any more money from today if you close the accounts. He'll know when the money is paid in. Your yearly account will pay out in the next few days, so at least we can stop him having access to that, and the monthly one."

I huff. "Yes, that's twenty-seven thousand he'll not get his hands on."

"Mrs Baxter, can you change the direct-debit instructions also?"

Gran nods.

I know Adam is going to be furious when he finds out about the accounts and the divorce.

"Mrs Bradshaw, I'll change the accounts today, but can the other stuff wait until after Christmas?"

"Why?" she asks.

"Because it nearly Christmas, and for once I'd like to be happy at Christmas."

"I really think it's best that you do it all now. You've left him, haven't you? And you're staying with a friend?"

"Yes, I've not been to the house for weeks now."

"He doesn't know where you're staying?" I shake my head. "So I think he's probably expecting you to do something, in fact I'm almost certain he is. I also think if you don't act now he'll become suspicious. Do you understand what I mean, Abigail?"

"Yes, of course. You're right."

"I'll start the proceedings immediately." She smiles warmly.

"Thank you," I reply as we get up to leave, but Gran starts speaking.

"Oh, by the way, how did Simone get on with her finals?"

Mrs Bradshaw beams at Gran, and picks up one of the photo frames from the desk.

"Here, take a look, Elizabeth," she says, passing her the picture frame. She's bursting with pride.

"Well, tell her congratulations from me."

I glance at the photo and see a pretty young woman dressed in a cap and gown. She's around twenty-eight or twenty-nine. You can tell it's her daughter, they're the spit of each other. I look at the solicitor, thinking she doesn't look old enough to have a daughter that age.

"I will, Elizabeth. Thank you. And she'll be joining me and Michael after the Christmas holidays. A criminal lawyer to add to our portfolio."

I don't say anything as I don't know her. They continue to chat for a few more minutes. Mrs Bradshaw moves from behind her desk to retrieve the photo frame, stares at it briefly, then puts it back on her desk. We say our goodbyes, and leave the office.

"Abigail, a word," Mrs Bradshaw say, calling me back.

"Yes."

Her expression is kind and warm. She smiles and placed her arm gently on my shoulder. I'm a little taken aback by the gesture. Her voice has changed.

"There's only seven days left until Christmas."

I nod, wondering where the conversation is going.

"I'm sure he'll not receive any correspondence until the New Year."

I smile.

"I knew your mother, Abigail. I went to school with her and your father. She was very beautiful … You look so much like her."

I hold in a breath.

"And you have the same kind traits she had."

I swallow. I'd no idea she knew my parents. She sees the surprise on my face and squeezes my hand tightly. "I'll work relentlessly for you to sort this out, and I'm sorry about mentioning Adam being narcissistic."

"So you think he could be?"

She nods. "Do some reading about it – their traits and the thing they do. I don't know much about it myself as I said, but I've taken some advice and been reading about it … the other things he's done to you. No remorse, as you said."

"I'll speak to Edward and ask him. He's a doctor. I'm sure he'll know. And if he doesn't, he'll know someone who does, I'm sure."

"That very sensible. And I know you said the police investigation threw up nothing, but let's see what Edward's brother Simon finds out."

"I'm meeting Simon on Boxing Day. If I get the chance, I'll speak to him. I'll ring you in the New Year, after Gran's birthday."

"Please, yes, the New Year. And if you don't mind, Abigail, I might bring Simone in on your case as she's a criminal lawyer."

"Yes, that's perfectly fine. Thank you. But I still don't want my gran knowing the details."

"I know you don't, but if it goes to court, which I'm presuming it will, then it'll come out."

"Yes, I somehow gathered that, but until then under no circumstances do I want her finding out. I need to be the one to tell her, at the right time, because I know it'll devastate her."

"I understand. Abigail. It's confidential. It'll not come from this office, I assure you."

"Good."

"Abigail, dear, are you ready?" Gran calls from reception.

"Yes, I'm coming."

I mime a thank you to Mrs Bradshaw and walk through to Gran. She smiles. I thread my arm through hers and we leave for the bank.

Chapter 10

The bank is surprisingly empty. I start towards the desk and
Gran follows.

"I'll do this, Gran. You take a seat."

She raises her eyes and I wink. She grins, taking a seat as
I'd asked. I think she likes the new me.

I reach the desk and clear my throat.

"Good morning. I'd like to see someone, please; I'd like to
close my current account," I say confidently

"Miss, you need to make an appointment."

I shake my head, standing firm.

"No, I'd like to see someone now, please," I repeat,
knowing I can't put if off for another day.

"As I said, miss, you need to make an appointment."

I shake my head again. I'm not leaving until I've stopped
that scumbag from taking anything more from me. I breathe in
deep.

Gran walks towards us – there's nothing wrong with her
hearing. I shake my head in annoyance. I have to start doing
things for myself. She sits back down and leaves me to speak.

"I said—"

Another clerk appears from behind a screen. "Stella, is
everything okay?"

"This customer wants to close her current account, but I told her—" Her eyes glance back at me.

"Can I stop you? If you don't get someone to see me now I'll remove my money from this bank."

She sniggers a little and my eyes go wide. Gran stands up.

"Stella, please take the customer's name," the other clerk says, trying to defuse the situation.

"Name," she says rudely.

"Baxter. Abigail Elizabeth Baxter."

She looks unconcerned and types my name into the computer.

"There are several accounts. Which one?" she snaps. Her eyes move to the other clerk standing next to her, then she glances back at me. She must have my bank details onscreen because her jaw is practically on the keyboard.

"Current account and savings account," I say calmly.

"Miss Baxter, I'm sorry," she says, returning her eyes to the screen. "Stella, I'll sort Miss Baxter out. Please move aside." And she nudges her with a withering look. Stella goes red. I shake my head.

"No, it's fine. I'm sure Stella can sort this out for me."

I'm feeling a little guilty as I know I'm taking my mood out on her. I've never used my name before to get my own way. Stella watches me.

"We've all had off days," I say, meaning it. "I'm sure Stella didn't mean to be rude, and neither did I."

We smile at each other.

"Okay, Miss Baxter, if you're sure. Would you like to go through to an office, or can I sort it out here for you?"

"Here will be fine, thank you. I'm in a bit of a rush."

She nods and I tell her what needs to be done. Then I wait for the paperwork. We're both quite amicable now, making small talk about Christmas and the weather. Finally, she asks if I'd like the balance for the new account. I nod and she prints a statement and hands it to me.

My brows raise when I see the number. "Stella, is that all the money from the old current account?"

"Yes. The savings account you asked me to close and the yearly accounts I've done, but there was nothing in those two accounts."

"Really?" I almost shout. "Nothing in either?"

She sits forward on her chair. "No, they were both empty." Her tone changes. "Should there have been?"

I look at the balance again. Twelve thousand pounds left in my current account, and zero in the yearly and savings ones. My head's whizzing. I can't calculate the exact numbers at the moment, but it's a bloody huge amount of money —two or three hundred thousand at least.

"Miss Baxter, are you okay? Do you want me to call the manager?"

I shake my head, knowing that even if she calls him, he can't do anything, because all those accounts are in joint names, so technically Adam's not broken the law. He's been crafty, leaving some money in the current account so I'd not become suspicious. But he knew I'd buy presents for Gran, and take money from the current account to pay for them.

"May I ask you when were the accounts emptied?"

She looks at the computer. "Two week ago. Let me just see if I can find the date. Ah, yes. Monday, the first of December, at …" She scrolls down. "12.30 p.m. Do you want to see?"

She placed her hand on the monitor to turn it towards me. I shake my head, remembering the date, and the approximate time. It was after the bust-up at the Lakes. Then I smashed my phone. He must still think I'm away.

"Miss Baxter, is there a problem?"

Gran pulls me away from my train of thought as she approaches the desk.

"Abigail, what's going on?" I just stare.

Stella looks at my gran.

"Abigail, what's the matter? Is there something wrong with your accounts?"

I don't know why I feel bewildered. I hadn't expected anything less from him and I know that it's always been about money. That's what he wanted and that's what he's got. But he's not going to take anymore. No matter what I do or say to him, how hard I hit or scream, nothing will enrage and provoke him more than not having access to my money. *Narcissistic*, that's what Mrs Bradshaw called him, whatever that means. I'm having no more. I want revenge for what he's done. Not because of the money, the house, any of that materialistic shit. But because the things he did to me – hurting me, making me miscarry – because he felt like it, with no thought, no remorse, and all to feed a habit inside his head.

I want revenge.

I want to take back what's mine – my self-respect, my dignity and my life – and to make him pay.

And, boy, will he pay.

I dearly wish I had that letter telling him he isn't entitled to the house, or the money. I'd watch his face drop, knowing there's nothing he can do about it.

I turn towards my gran. "It's what I expected, Gran. He's taken nearly the lot."

She sighs heavily. "But it's only money, and he can't do anything else now."

Stella looks on at us in puzzlement. Gran squeezes my hand.

"Shall we go?"

I nod, wondering if this will be the end of it. Or will he want more?

"You have Edward now, Abbie."

I smile. "Yes, I do, Gran, and I love him," I say, forgetting where I am. I look at Stella and she smiles. I thank her for her help. She's kind and says she hopes it works out fine.

As we make our way outside, it dawns on me that I've got no money or cards.

"Gran, I've no money and I wanted to buy Edward's Christmas present before going to the doctor's. I need to go back inside."

"Something nice from Forbes?" she asks.

"A watch. And I want to get it engraved."

She reaches into her bag. I shake my head, but she says, "When have you ever asked me for anything?"

"Never."

"Exactly. So take this card and get your presents. It's not a gift – you can pay me back when your new card arrives."

"Thank you, Gran. You know I will."

"I know, Abbie. Now off you go. And have a long chat with him when you get home. And I'll see you on Wednesday at the deli, usual time. And you can pick up your hamper for his parents."

I smile, which shocks me, as I was going to do all those things anyway. I'm not going to mope around or cry, because I don't feel anything at all for Adam. In fact, he's dead to me. I'm not scared because he can't possibly hurt me anymore than he already has. I'm mending, and coming back fighting. I like this new me. No, absolutely love her. And nothing on this earth is going to spoil my Christmas with Edward.

Gran kisses me on the cheek. Then my phone rings. I smile in hope of who it's going be, and I'm not disappointed.

"It's Edward."

"I leave you to it then."

She nods and walks off in the direction of the deli. I stand for a few seconds watching this spritely lady crossing the road.

"Abbie?"

"How are you?" he asks, his voice laced with concern.

"I actually feel fine."

"Did you sort out what you needed to?"

"Hmm … can I explain tonight?" I don't want to discuss it over the phone, especially not on the high street, which is busy now.

"Of course."

"Thank you."

"Where are you anyway?"

"On the high street, just doing some Christmas shopping. And I was going to get something for our tea. Anything you fancy?"

"Mmm … Let me see. You!" he shouts, and I giggle.

"Be serious!"

"Oh, I am!" he says, and I'm sure I'm blushing.

And feeling brave because I'm on the phone, I answer, "Okay, me it is then. Would you like salad or veg with that, sir?"

He growls seductively, catapulting goosebumps over me. He stops suddenly as a voice in the background says, "Mr Scott, we're ready, sir."

"I won't be a minute; I just need to finish this important call," he replies firmly.

"Oh, sorry, sir. I didn't realise you were on your phone. I'll tell the team." There's a brief silence, then Edward says thank you and I hear the door close.

"Are you in theatre?" I ask, shocked, but delighted that I'm his *important call*.

"Yes."

"Well, I'd better let you go then."

"Not before we've discussed what I want for dessert," he says smoothly.

I can't believe I'm having this conversation with him on a packed high street.

"Edward, get off the phone and back to work. Stop chit-chatting to me about your stomach."

"I'm thinking about you now, Abigail, not my stomach," he murmurs.

"Well, don't if you have surgery."

He laughs hard, and I think he's remembering our last conversation about him thinking of me at work, and what he said it did to him.

"I'll see you tonight. We can talk, eat and do whatever you like for dessert."

"Date," he replies quickly, knowing he's got his own way. But I don't mind in the slightest. In fact, I have quite a large grin on my face, knowing I'm going to enjoy dessert as well. "I'll see you tonight, sweetheart." I hear him breathe and almost feel it on the side of my neck.

"Mmm ... bye then." He hangs up and I have the most ridiculous smile on my face as I enter Forbes.

As I enter I'm greeted by a man in maroon top hat and tails.

"Good morning, miss. Welcome to Forbes," he says formally.

He's standing next to a forty- or fifty-foot Christmas tree. The branches are adorned with everything from teddy bears to perfume. And the smell that's wafting around the store is Christmas itself. Cinnamon, mulled wine and pine. I'm enveloped by nostalgia but, of course, that's the point – these multi-million-pound stores know exactly how to put on a show.

"May I direct you to a department?" he asks.

"No, I'm fine thank you." He nods and greets the next person.

I wander down the centre, which has smaller aisles off to the side leading to counters selling all sorts, from decorations and leather handbags to sweets and the hottest new toys. I hear children giggling excitedly, dragging their parents to the counters and begging them for the toys on display. My heart swells and my smile widens as I gaze upon this shoppers' paradise.

It turns out to be exhausting. I dash around Forbes while the engraver finishes the inscription on Edward's watch. I've managed to get everyone's presents – a pair of beautiful diamond earrings for Gran; a friendship bracelet for Alison; a crystal vase for Glenda and William, and a nice single malt for Tom. I return to the engraver, and sit almost in a trance as I watch all the shoppers buying presents, and the children squealing with delight, dragging their parents towards the stairs to the second floor and Santa's grotto. I smile at everyone who passes me and I must look a little simple. But I don't care because, finally, I'm *one* of those happy people.

I leave Forbes, and it's as if I've walked out onto a film set. Snow has started to fall. Children laugh and skid in the snow and there are lots of people dashing around, laden with boxes and bags. And I'm one of them.

I've bought some lovely food for our tea – fillet steak, sautéed garlic mushrooms, chef's salad, crusty warm bread, a bottle of nice wine that the butcher recommended, and lots of other beautiful nibbles. I did get a dessert. I couldn't resist the lemon cheesecake; the lady at the counter laughed at me when I told her it had talked to me, told me to take it home.

I've spent an absolute fortune, and for once I don't feel guilty. I've even bought something for myself. Well, I say for myself, but I think Edward will enjoy it far more. Just in case he doesn't want the cheesecake.

I dash to the car park at the back of the deli and place one bag on the passenger seat and the rest in the boot. Then I lock the door and head into the deli via the stock room.

"Hello again," says Ted. "You've just missed your gran. She's ordered your hamper. I thought it was Wednesday you were picking it up."

"Yes, Ted, Wednesday."

"Oh, I'm glad. She's asked for a large deluxe one, and for things to be put in for children and toddlers. I'll have to order a few things in." I shake my head. "Is that not right, Abigail?"

"No, that's fine, Ted. If that's what she ordered." The deluxe hampers are at least four times more than I gave her, probably more with the extras.

"I'll have it delivered to you, Abbie. They're quite large and heavy. I wouldn't want you hurting yourself." He pushes a pad towards me. "Put your name and address on there for me, and I'll sort it. Give me your mobile number as well, and I'll make sure they ring you before delivering it."

"Thanks, Ted," I say as I scribble down Edward's address and my phone number.

"Anything else, Abbie?"

"Please can I have a cheese-and-salmon bagel and latte to go?"

He strips out the page and places it on the orders spike at the back of the counter.

My tummy rumbles as the latte steams, and the bagel warms. We almost argue about paying, though he wins and I return my purse to my bag.

I go back to the car and head of towards the doctor's, singing out loud to a very smooth and talented Mr Bublé as I go.

His voice is like Edward's – tempting – and my mouth waters, though not because of the song but because of the delicious smell coming from the brown paper wrapper containing my bagel. I pull into a parking space and leave the engine running, just as Mr Bublé finishes his song, wishing everyone a very merry Christmas.

"And you!" I say aloud, reaching for my bagel and devouring it like I've not eaten for months. I lick my lips, savouring the last bite, and pick up my coffee. Then I reach for the gift I've bought Edward. I open the box, turning the Rolex over and read the inscription on the back. I'm going to write a poem in his card but I need time to think about the words. I return the watch to its lush box with a smile.

It's quite warm in the car now. I open the window to the passenger side slightly. I've ten minutes to spare, so I just sit back and savour the taste of my hot latte.

Chapter 11

I'm suddenly distracted as a car pulls in next to me and stops abruptly. I glance to the side and hear shouting from inside. My eyes widen as the door opens.

"Shut that thing up now."

I cringe. Adam gets out and looks around the car park it's empty of people so he shouts into the car again and I hear the cries of a baby and Nicky's voice trying to soothe it.

"Are you getting out of the fucking car? I've already told you I only had five minutes." He glares. "It's bloody ridiculous that you can't drive yourself!"

"I'm sorry … I'm sorry, shush," she says, trying to stop the baby from crying. "Come on, sweetheart. Shush,"

"For fuck's sake! Stop pissing about and just get out of the car."

The door opens at the back and Nicky slowly gets out. She looks dreadful – drained, dark circles around her eyes, her hair scraped up in a ponytail. She pulls down her jumper over her arms, but not before I see the purple bruises. I close my eyes, thinking how this woman I've detested for so long is standing there looking like a zombie. Her voice is weak and apprehensive; she seems almost too scared to speak.

"Adam, can you please get the baby? It hurts when I lift the car seat," she asks feebly, but he stares at her with disgust, as if she's just asked him to do something dreadful.

"You wanted the fucking thing, you look after it."

My hand is on my mouth; I feel torn, knowing he's hurting her, just like he once hurt me. I suddenly have an urge to help her, though I can't rationalise why because I owe her nothing.

She opens the passenger door. He stands watching her, waiting, and looking at his watch. I can see how panicked she looks. My eyes close as he walks around to her door, while doing nothing, as if frozen. My heart's beating ten to the dozen. I don't want to look, but the baby's cries force me to and the sight pains me. She removes the car seat, struggling to lift it. Haunting memories consume me immediately as I see the pink blanket covering the little helpless bundle, and a matching bonnet on its head. I try ever so hard to look away, but I can't, because I'm scared he's going to hurt the baby. It's going to fall, and that he's not going to help.

She's defenceless, staring at the baby, trying to protect it from him. I reach for the door handle, knowing I couldn't live with myself if she fell and harmed the child. She stumbles and my heart's in my mouth as I think she's going to fall with the car seat. I pull the door and open it. I don't think about myself; my focus is on the car seat and what lies inside.

"Look at the state of you. You'd better get your act together or we're finished. God knows why I even went with you!"

She's frozen. Her hands shake, which makes the car seat wobble. His face is screwed tight, and he talks through gritted teeth. "Stop messing over that!" He glares at the baby. His baby.

My heart races with repulsion. He moves in close to her face.

"I'm telling you now ..." Then suddenly he straightens and smiles, and I'm mesmerised by his behaviour, remembering how manipulative he is. A couple are leaving through the doors and making their way to the car park. He'd certainly not want anyone to hear what he was truly like. I see him looking over towards them. His body language changes as they approach a car close by. His voice is now slimy. He watches them, but glances back at Nicky as though to warn her to keep her mouth shut. Lies pour from his poisonous lips. I want to be sick as he continues with the lies and untruths.

"Look, sweetheart, let me help you. I told you not to carry that car seat. You'll hurt yourself. Shush, little one," he wheedles, loud enough that the couple will hear, as if he's the doting father and partner.

"Oh, she's beautiful," says the woman. "What's her name?"

He smiles at them both. I'm unable to move my eyes away from the cunning, evil person now holding onto the car seat. His free hand goes towards the baby's cheek. Nicky looks terrified as he smiles and strokes it with his finger down it cheek. Her face is stunned, as if he's touching the baby for the first time. I wonder whether he's harmed the baby, or threatened to.

He opens his mouth to reveal the baby's name. I don't want to hear because knowing would be a connection too far. But I'm unable to block the sound out even with the radio, and I daren't close the window because then they'll know someone's inside the car next to them, heard the conversation. I start humming to myself, but it's too late and he replies with all the charm in the world.

"Abigail."

I throw my hand to my mouth. Bile hits the back of my throat. Nicky's eyes fly towards Adam's in shock, but he continues to smile.

"That's a lovely name, isn't it, Alan?" the woman says, smiling at her husband.

"Yes, we thought so, didn't we, dear?" Adam says, looking at Nicky.

She nods robotically with a weak smile, but I think she's too scared to say anything different. This surely can't be her doing. Because who in their right mind would consent to giving your ex's name to your baby? Not that she appears to be in her right mind.

Thoughts catapult around my head but then everything comes to a screeching halt as the next sentence leaves his lips.

"She's named after someone close to us who recently died."

My thoughts turn dark. I see him squeezing Nicky's hand until she nods in response. Oh my God, what did he mean?

He's sick, perverted. My hand slowly pulls the door closed. It makes a noise and he turns in my direction. He stares straight at the car, but he can't see me. I feel sick seeing his face, hearing that bullshit, and the mind games he's playing with Nicky. He's fucking twisted.

Nicky's head's down in a submissive way, and she reminds me so much of how I used to be. She needs to leave him and take the baby before he harms it.

"It'll be our turn next week, won't it, love?" Alan says to the woman, smiling, and he's genuinely pleased. She raises her eyes, and shrugs in agreement. And that's how it should be, not like what I experienced, or what Nicky's going through. It should never be like that for anyone.

"Come on, dear," he adds. "It's getting cold."

They walking towards their car and I'm torn. Do I get out, do I stay, or do I just go? Adam's still glaring at her, but her head is down looking at the baby. His expression is one of disgust, and I know what's waiting for her tonight. He snaps, nearly throwing the car seat. She gasps, grabbing it quickly with one hand, soothing the baby he's just startled. His face is flat. There's no care, no concern for his actions.

"You can get a taxi home. I'm going back to work."

"But—"

She stops looking at him. His body language is aggressive, something I'm all too familiar with.

"What, you want to argue here?" He raises his hand, because there's no one around to see his behaviour. But I can see. I can see all too well. That expression on his face, that vacant look, as if he's just pulled into the car park and none of this has happened. Mrs Bradshaw's words float over me with an icy chill. No remorse. No concept of anyone's feelings apart from his own. I'm desperate to get out of the car and confront him, to ask why. Why he's called his baby Abigail. What sick mind game is he playing? But if I do, he'll know I'm back, and I don't want that. I breathe deeply, knowing he's fucking with my head again. She's almost cowering.

"I fucking thought not. And register that as Abigail Lord, got it?"

She nods nervously. He grunts and gets back into his car, driving off, leaving her standing in the snow with the baby. She's struggling to hold the car seat, and I've no choice – I have to help. I get out, pull my hood as far over my face as I can to disguise myself, as I don't want a confrontation with her. And I don't want to look at her, because deep down I know it's not her. She's broken, like I was. Her past actions are distant to me now. Adam has probably fed her bullshit about me, said I was to blame, and she believed him. And why wouldn't she? I did.

But I still can't look at the baby, because that hurts too much, as though a knife is being thrust through my heart, twisting, ripping, pulling and wakening my thoughts. Thoughts that I've tried to bury deep down.

I know I'm not doing it to help her. I'm doing it for that helpless little thing, who didn't ask to be born to a father who's evil. I leave the car and walk quickly towards her.

"Here let me help you."

She nods pathetically, not looking at me. I could be absolutely anyone as I take hold of the car seat. My hand is almost touching hers but I don't think about that I look straight ahead towards the entrance. The doors automatically open and two paramedics come out. I grab one of their hands and speak in a low voice.

"Can you please help her?"

I've made a mistake. I can't do this. My emotions are getting the better of me. Because now I want to scream at Nicky.

I need to leave. I'm confused.

The paramedic looks at me strangely. "Please," I say, widening my eyes and looking at the bruises on Nicky's neck. The woman's eyes follow mine and then return to me.

I close my eyes tight. And no matter how much I want to ask Nicky why she didn't stand up for me, why she didn't help me, I just can't bring myself to ask those question. And one thing Edward has taught me over these past months is that jealously is an ugly trait.

The paramedic sees the anguish on my face and addresses Nicky.

"Miss, are you okay?" Nicky still has her head down, staring at the baby. "Your friend says—" I shake my head. She's no friend of mine. "Do you need some help?"

Nicky remains mute.

I remove my hand from the car seat and it slips to one side, forcing the woman to take hold of it, freeing me to leave. I make my way forward, moving further away from the entrance. The other paramedic pulls at my hand and starts to speak as I turn my head towards him. My hood slips just as Nicky looks up. Our eyes meet in silence. She casts her eyes back at the baby and I freeze momentarily. Her face is a shadow of secrets from the world, but I know those secrets. She stumbles towards me and I step back, not wanting anything to do with her. I've done my bit.

"I'm sorry," she whispers.

I turn and walk away, hearing the words in the empty space, wondering if she means them or not. But I don't look back. I hear a thud but still I don't turn. I've done what I can; the rest is up to her.

"Andrew, fetch a doctor. She's collapsed." Her words echo off the wall.

I breathe in deeply, but continue inside towards the reception desk. I give my name and wait to be called through to see the doctor.

My name's called and I enter the doctor's room.

"Good morning." She smiles. "Please take a seat. What can I do for you?"

"I've come for a check-up, to see if the infection has cleared."

She smiles, and checks the computer screen.

"It appears to have; all your blood results are back to normal."

"Thank you."

"Anything else, Abigail?"

"Umm, yes. May I leave a urine sample to be tested for pregnancy?"

"Do you think you might be pregnant?" I shrug. "When was your last period?"

"Early last week."

"So what makes you think you might be pregnant?"

I explain what's happened and that Edward's insisted I get the test done, that he wants to be a hundred per cent sure this time, with him being a doctor and all. Her eyes raise. Then she enquires a little more and it turns out she actually knows him. I smile, not really sure if I'm pleased that my doctor knows my boyfriend. But she cottons on.

"All consultations are confidential, Abigail."

I close the door to her surgery. The doctor's agreed to the test but I think she's only humouring Edward. Still, as I head towards reception, I grin, knowing he's going to be ecstatic about the pill working. I'm reminded of his words before I left, and the suggestive tone in his voice.

I hand in my sample. I'm told the results will be available after Christmas and they'll phone me to make an appointment. I leave my new mobile number and head down the corridor towards the car park, thinking nothing more about it.

Then I hear a commotion in the corridor near the entrance. A woman lies on a stretcher with a red blanket over her. A lady is holding her hand, and a man is talking to a police officer and holding a baby that's wrapped in a pink blanket and wearing a matching bonnet. I hold back to eavesdrop on the conversation.

"No, she's not going back there. We'll take the baby home with us."

I breathe a sigh of relief, knowing that they're taking the baby home with them. And I know that the man and woman are Nicky's parents. He continues talking to the police; his face is like thunder, but he's holding it together for now, as the baby sleeps in his arms. Nicky lies motionless on the stretcher while her mum comforts her.

"Why didn't you not tell us before? Look at you. Look at your baby. You've not even named her," she says, crying as she strokes the side of her face. "Come on, Nicky. It's over. You're not going back to him." She continues to fuss over her, telling her she's safe.

Nicky smiles at her mum, closes her eyes and whispers, "Mum, I'm calling her Sarah, after Grandma."

I make my way quickly past and a chill runs down my spine as I think about what Adam's doing. I reach my car and sit in a daze, wondering why I feel as I do. I should feel happy that's Nicky's reaping what she's sowed, but I don't. And I'm glad I don't feel bitter towards her, that I feel empathy for another human being, because if I didn't, that would make me no better than him. It would make me a monster.

I start the car and try to stop thinking about the baby, because I know she's safe with her grandparents. And by the looks on their faces, there's no way on earth that they'd allow her or their daughter return to Adam. That gives me some peace. Still, I want to know why he wanted to register the baby's name as Abigail.

I put the radio on to distract myself as I make my way back to the house, although the question is still nagging away at the back of my mind. I want answers, answers I don't have.

I pull up at the gates. They open without my needing the key code. I move forward and up towards the house. The BMW is on the drive. He's home early. The door opens and I'm greeted by a smile, and Shadow, as I pull the car to a stop. I gaze at him standing there, smiling, looking so pleased to see me, and I know I have the rest of my life to look forward to with this honest, flawless, compassionate man making his way towards me.

I hold my breath, as I know what I have to do – leave it be. Not dwell on Adam or why he's done this or that, because that's exactly what he wants. To control me with his mind games. But no more. I've learned the hard way, and I'm not returning.

I'm going to tell Edward everything.

My door opens and his words float over me, hugging me like a safety blanket. I'm completely consumed by his love.

"I've missed you today," he says, kissing me tenderly on the lips.

I smile into his kiss, holding him close, closing my eyes, never wanting these feelings to leave. These feelings of love, warmth, hope, safety. I squeeze him tight.

"Hey, what's this? Are you all right?"

I nod and stare into his eyes. Kind eyes that hold my gaze, speak his words, his love. He gently brushes my cheek with his finger and places a stray strand of hair behind my ear. My heart melts under his tender touch.

His head tilts to one side as if he's puzzled.

I'm unable to answer so I nod, because I've no doubt, no doubt whatsoever, that he's mending me.

Chapter 12

I awake as the bed dips to my side. His breath floats over my face like a warm summer breeze before he releases an alluring moan. There's another dip as he straddles me and places his hands either side of my shoulders.

I slowly open my eyes, blinking as a drop of water falls from his wet hair onto my nose. He smiles leisurely, noticing that I've seen that dark, hooded look in his eyes, and I know what's coming next. He's naked. His muscular torso and arms hold me fast, and for his pleasure. He sees me staring at how aroused he is and seems pleased with himself as he slowly bends forward, kisses my mouth, then teases my neck with his lips.

"Good morning, Abbie," he whispers. "Are we getting up?"

I hear the suggestion in his voice as he devours my neck and lazily moves to my breasts. The tingling starts in my toes and moves to my core. My eyes close with pleasure. He's not playing fair this morning; he knows what that does to me. Knows I can't say no to him when he kisses my neck; it's my weak spot. His hand reaches down and pulls the duvet from my body, and a growl leaves his throat. I pant as he nuzzles and suckles at my neck. I know I'm so easy, that I can't resist him. I never say no and, of course, that's what he likes, but I need to try and sound as if I'm not so desperate.

"Good morning, Edward. You're very eager today." I keep my voice as stoic as I can but my body has already awakened to his touch. He merely nods and waits. "I was hoping for a lie-in this morning." His eyes raise, as if to say, *Really?* He knows I won't say no and he can tell I'm trying my best not to laugh. "But I can't see any possibility of that now. Can you?"

"No, Abbie, I can't," he says wickedly. I squeal as he grabs me and flips me over on to my tummy. One arm goes under my waist and pulls me upwards so that I'm on my knees with my forearms leaning on the bed. He applies gentle pressure at the back of my neck to hold me down.

"One of my favourite positions!" he whispers seductively into my ear.

My heart races in anticipation of what he's going to do to me. I yelp, shocked as his hand comes down on my bottom firmly, but not hard, making it sting. Then he massages over the smack. His eager mouth kisses my back and his teeth graze my skin as he continues rubbing and squeezing my bottom. His voice is low and gravelled.

"God, I want to spank your arse."

I feel confused, unsure, a little scared of where it may lead.

"Did you like that?" he asks breathlessly.

I don't answer. His hand goes under my waist again and he pulls me up onto my knees with my back against his chest. He continues kissing and grazing his teeth against the side of my neck. His breath flows softly over me, hypnotising me, compelling me to give myself willingly. He cups one of my breasts, twizzles my erect nipple between his fingers and thumb. His other hand slides down my body and cups my sex, enticing me.

"You did like it, didn't you?" He inhales, answering for me. "You're soaking wet already."

I gasp, knowing I'm unable to answer one way or another, because he's turning me on so much now. He knows exactly which spot to touch, how to send me into a trance of pleasure.

"Answer me, Abbie," he says, increasing the pressure.

My eyes roll with the sensation.

"Y-Yes," I say.

"Do you want more?"

I nod.

"Do you want me to finger you?"

My head spins. I don't know what to say, and I don't know what he really means – to continue doing this, which is bringing me to orgasm so quickly, or to spank me?

"I don't want you to hurt me, Edward."

"I'd never hurt you. Now lie back down as you were."

And I do, feeling really mixed up. I'm now in the same position as before. His voice has grown firmer.

"Push your bottom up higher, Abbie."

But I don't do it so he lifts it for me. Again, a low growl leaves his throat and I know he's turned on. I don't want him to spank me, though I feel I can't say no. He continues moaning and places his hands firmly on my hips. One hand glides up my back, then into my hair. He wraps it gently around the palm of his hand, tugging on it slightly so my head moves to the side.

"I want to watch your face."

Again his lips find the side of my neck, and he whispers softly in my ear, telling me what he's going to do.

"I'm going to finger you – make you scream for more as you come for me." He breathes, slides his fingers between my legs, inserts one and begins to circle it. Another finger slides in, pushing deeper. I moan, knowing I'm going to orgasm soon, but aware he's going to spank me. I screw my eyes tight shut.

"You like this, don't you?" he rasps.

I inhale, unsure what's happening to me. My body's taking over my mind. His fingers increase in speed, pushing in firm. As he increases the pressure delicious goosebumps prickle my body. I feel his hand move upwards. He inhales sharply and brings his hand down onto the cheek of my bottom. He groans with pleasure, but for me it hurts; it's not arousing, and those nice feelings suddenly leave me. I feel trapped.

I try to move my head, but he breathes deep, increases the speed of his fingers, his thumb is firm on my clitoris. I stare at his face. His eyes are closed and he looks lost, but I need him to stop. I move my hand between my legs and try to move his hand, but this only adds to his excitement.

"You want it again?" he says, and I can hear the excitement in his voice.

I'm screaming internally, but he can't hear me. His hand comes down again hard.

"Fuck, Abbie," he shouts. He removes his fingers and moves his hands swiftly to my hips. "I can't wait. I need to fuck you." He's almost barking.

He looks at me, but doesn't see me, he can't see that I want him to stop, that I've said no. He slams into me. He's very hard, and I cry out from the sting as I stretch.

"I need to fuck you hard, baby. Tell me, Abbie. Tell me to fuck you hard and fast."

I close my eyes tight shut, trying to stop the flashbacks.

"Tell me. Come on, tell me."

My hands begin to shake and my heart races. Is he the same as Adam? Does he want to hurt me? Because, right now he is. He pounds hard and deep, stretching, forcing himself into me, moaning my name with every thrust, and I can't get the words out of my mouth. They're stuck in my throat, but I need him to stop.

"Come, Abbie. Come on," he shouts, and there's impatience in his tone. He pulls at my nipples then gropes my breasts. His other hand sinks hard into my hip. Tears start to course my cheeks, but he can't see them, he doesn't know what I'm feeling. It's like he's in a trance, and I wonder have I got him so wrong, why is he doing this to me.

"Abbie," he shouts, as he slaps my bottom again.

"Stop!" I scream, throwing my head back. My hands slap at his.

He freezes, as if he's just released what he's doing, and pulls out of me quickly as my voice echoes around the room.

"Stop. Stop."

He looks shocked, scared, and he holds his head down.

"Abbie, I'm so sorry," he whispers, but my tears continue as I stare at him, trying to work out if he's telling the truth. He lifts his head and his eyes meet mine.

"Please. I'm sorry. I'd nev—"

I shake my head, but he pulls me into his arms and holds me tightly. His hands are shaking.

"Please, Abbie. Please don't think I'd hurt you."

He moves me away to look at my face, and I don't know what to believe. His eyes look pained, as if me he speaks the truth. His finger wipes a tear. "Please, believe me," he whispers. "What have I done to you?"

My head's still shaking. I don't want to dredge all those memories to the forefront of my mind again. And still I wonder why he did that. What made him want to?

"I'm sorry," I manage weakly. I push his hands away and move off the bed. He's just brought Adam right back, reminding me of what he was like – hurting me, hitting me, making me submit until I cried.

I take a deep breath. I want to go to the bathroom and be on my own. I knew Edward wanted more from me, but I thought he understood what I'd been through. My subconscious is nattering away, pecking at my head. *He's just like Adam.*

Tears sting my eyes as I walk past him, my head down, because I don't want him to see that I'm crying because of what he's just done to me. I feel his eyes on me and I turn to look at him. He holds his head down and speaks quietly.

"Please talk to me. Tell me what you're feeling. Please don't bottle it up like before. I'm sorry I got carried away. I thought you wanted it because you didn't say no."

I stare at him he bites the inside of his cheek, his head tilted to one side. I close my eyes and take a deep breath.

"I can't … and why? Why would you want to hurt me?"

"I didn't want to hurt you, Abbie. I wanted to give you pleasure," he answers quickly.

"What? By hitting me?"

"No," he says firmly. "Not hitting you. There's a difference between spanking and hitting. I'd never hit you – you do know that, don't you?" But his remark is flat and I feel a little trapped, as though this kind of sex is normal for him. Did he honestly think I'd enjoy it? I think he should have discussed it with me first.

His next comment knocks me for six.

"Do you want to leave, Abbie?"

A tear falls onto my cheek at the thought of leaving him, because I love him so much, but I'm unsure why he'd ask me that. Does he want me to leave just because I don't want to do the things he does in the bedroom?

My head is swimming – I know he's kind, that he shows me so much tenderness, but now all of a sudden he wants to spank me. He says he's falling for me, but has never told me he loves me. And I don't know what to believe and I feel scared because now I'm thinking, *Is he like Adam? Have I got him so wrong?*

I walk towards the door that leads into the dressing room, and he offers me his hand.

"No," I reply quietly.

He looks stunned but I feel I need to leave. I can't think straight with him here. So I go into the dressing room and dress quickly. I'm about to leave just as the door opens. I move forward to walk out, but he quickly enters and closes the door behind him, blocking my way.

He shakes his head. "Don't, Abbie. Don't leave," he says nervously.

"I can't do those things you're asking me to do, Edward. I'm sorry but I have to go."

"No. No you don't. I'll not let you. I can't let you." He sounds desperate.

Tears well my eyes. "You can't stop me, Edward."

His stare is intense; his eyes haven't moved from mine. He closes them quickly, then stands to one side.

"No, I can't stop you if that's what you want," he whispers, sounding defeated.

He opens the door. I freeze, knowing I don't want to go.

He walks towards me and my lip quivers as he holds me to him.

"Don't leave me, Abbie. Please."

And I want to scream. I don't know what to do or say. Deep down in my heart I know he wouldn't hurt me, because surely I'd have left by now otherwise. And I certainly wouldn't be feeling so anxious at the thought of going. Plus, when he asked me if he could spank me, I didn't answer, so I suppose my silence was misunderstood as a yes. I hold my head down, but he lifts my chin to his face.

"He was nasty to you and I knew that, but I just got carried away. I'm sorry. I'll never do it again, I promise."

I nod.

"Were you scared?"

"Yes," I admit after a brief silence.

He holds his head down. "I'm ashamed of myself. Abbie."

I know it's the truth. I can tell by his eyes. They're telling me he's sorry, confused, sad.

"Do you want to leave?" His expression tells me to stay. His hands cup my face and he moves his forehead against mine. Then he breathes in deep. "I'd be lost without you."

I feel the same.

"I'm not leaving Edward, and I'd be lost without you too. But we should have talked about it first."

"Yes, I know."

"I know why you did it, and I freaked out, but I do trust you. I know that you'd never hurt me, and I'm not saying I'd never do anything like that, but I need time."

"You mean that?" he asks softly.

"Yes."

His arms come around me, and I know then that I'm going to spend the rest of my life with him. His lips move to mine, then slowly across my cheek towards my ear.

"I love you," he whispers.

My eyes open wide; did I hear him right? did he just tell me *he loves me*. I look at him, stunned by his admission.

"Edward, did you …"

"Yes, Abbie, I love you," he repeats.

We hold each other close and kiss. And I feel his love as he glides his hands around my back, pulling me even closer.

"Let me make love to Abbie. Let me show you."

He leads me towards the bed and starts to gently undress me, then lowers me down softly and lies on top of me. His lips never leave my skin as he slowly places himself inside me, whispering all the while that he loves me as he takes me into his world, our world, of sublime pleasure.

Chapter 13

My eyes open suddenly. I'm warm and naked again, but alone. I know I've been dreaming about Adam, although I can't remember the details. I rub my face and sit up against the headboard.

I spend five minutes mulling things over. I feel a little guilty, thinking I've over-analysed it all, because Edward is nothing like Adam. Yes, he got carried away, but so have I in the throes of passion.

I put it down to the fact that I'm a little nervous about what's been happening these past days. Seeing Nicky at the doctor's. Adam's behaviour towards her. Him insisting the baby be registered with the name Abigail. That left a horrible taste in my mouth – it's the behaviour of someone who's seriously disturbed, maybe. And then there's what he said to the couple in the car park – *She's named after someone close to us who recently died.* Edward called it a bogus delusion, and said I shouldn't dwell on it, that he'd protect me.

I know Edward was shocked when I told him about what happened in the car park, but as ever he tried to cover it up. We've talked at length about what Mrs Bradshaw had said, about Adam being narcissistic. I've asked Edward about it several times but he's held back, saying, he doesn't know much about the disorder. I suspect he knows more than he's letting on, though. I know he's spoken to Simon, but about what, I'm uncertain, because every time I ask he changes the subject; he simply won't be drawn on the matter – just keeps telling me it'll be sorted soon and not to worry anymore.

I make my way to the bathroom and take a shower – washing Adam out of my thoughts and watching him swirl down the plug hole. I'm getting better at this by the day.

I dress and head downstairs. Shadow bounces over to meet me on the bottom step, wagging his tail, panting and jumping around until I've stroked him.

"Good morning, Shadow," I say, and as he barks likes he's answering me. "Where's Edward?" He barks again, then trots down the hallway towards the kitchen, looking behind to ensure I'm following. The doorbell rings and I go to answer it. Shadow barks and runs past me to the door.

"Shadow, stop." Edward's behind me. "It's a delivery for you."

"How do you know?"

"They came through on the intercom in the kitchen." He says as he opens the door.

"Morning, Abbie," says Ted. "I thought I'd drop your hamper off – there's no way you'd have managed it."

I roll my eyes, knowing Gran must have had it rammed full of all sorts.

Edward looks puzzled.

"It's for your parents, for us to take on Boxing Day."

"There was no need to do that."

Shadow barks again and looks down the drive. I pat his head to calm him, but he takes no notice and continues looking towards the gates. Then he bolts off down the drive, snarling. Edward calls him back, but to my surprise he doesn't stop; he continues hurtling down the drive with his hackles up. He stops abruptly, skidding next to the gates, and sniffs the ground, then the air. Then he turns quickly and launches himself into the bushes as if he's found a scent.

Edward places two fingers in his mouth and whistles sharply three times. Shadow flies out of the bush, covered in a dusting of snow. He looks towards Edward, then back at the bush before starting heading back towards us. He sits in front of Edward, his eyes bright, waiting for his command, then barks. He suddenly looks like the dog Edward has described – highly trained, obedient, and doing his job. Edward bends and pats him on the head, then looks down towards the gates.

"Good boy, Shadow."

Edward takes my hand, gesturing me inside, along with Ted and the hamper.

"What was he barking at?" I ask, a little taken aback.

"Just a rabbit probably. They tease him in the garden. He's not as fast as he used to be before his accident," he answers a little too slowly. And it makes me wonder, because I've seen Shadow with rabbits, seagulls and birds, and, yes, he barked at them, but didn't chase and snarl like that, but I don't dwell on it.

I bend down towards him.

"Poor boy," I say, stroking him. "Those naughty rabbits."

Edward raises an eye as I giggle, but Ted stares at Shadow, as if a little wary of him.

"Wow, that's some well-trained dog you have there, mate," Ted says. Edward just nods. "Where do you want me to put the hamper, Abbie?"

"Just there, Ted, please," I reply, pointing to the ottoman.

"Would you like a coffee?"

"No, I best not. I've quite a few deliveries to make. You know how busy it gets this time of year."

"Of course. Thanks for dropping it off. You've saved me a journey into town."

"No probs."

Edward offers Ted a tip.

"No, mate. Cheers anyway – all part of the service. Plus, Abbie's gran would kill me if she thought I'd taken a tip for the delivery."

"Ted, you're still very old school," I say with a laugh.

"Yep, that's me – old-school Ted. Anyway, I don't make the rules," he says, laughing, as he walks out through the door. "You both have a nice Christmas."

"You too, Ted, and your family."

He waves and gets back into the small brown delivery van. Baxter's Deli is written in gold script that flows beautifully around the vintage van. I smile, remembering going out with Ted when I was little. People waved at us and I think Baxter's has become a little iconic now.

Edward walks outside and heads over to Ted. Edward speaks. Ted shakes his head. Then they both looking down the drive. Edward nods and comes back in. He presses a button for the gates to open, then locks the front door.

"Coffee," I say, and we walk towards the kitchen. "Are you going into work today?"

"Yes."

"What time?"

"About ten. Why?" he asks, puzzled.

"I need a lift back to my house. I'd like to pick up somethings for the party tonight."

"What things?"

"Shoes, makeup, perfume. I can't go wearing my wellies or boots under that beautiful dress you bought me, can I?"

"Oh, I don't know. You might start a new trend – country meets society."

"Ha-ha, very funny. Well, are you going to give me a lift or not?"

"I'd rather go with you," he says a little too firmly for my liking.

"Why?"

"Because," he replies flatly.

"That's not an answer."

"It's the best you're getting," he says turning his back to me and filling the coffee cups with hot water. I stare at his back, knowing he meant it, but I'm curious as to why he doesn't want me to go back to the house on my own. So I test the water out.

"So when I move back home, Ed—"

His head turns sharply, stopping me in my tracks.

"When you what?" he almost shouts.

"When I move back home. I mean ... I can't stay here forever, can I?"

"Why?" he says.

We stare at each other like two stubborn mules, but he gives in first. "Is it because of this morning?"

I shake my head. I thought we'd cleared that up.

His eyes raise. "Well?"

"God, no, not because of that. We talked about that, cleared it up. You explained and I understood."

"So why?"

I shrug.

"Do you want to leave?"

"I'm not leaving, Edward; I'm just giving us some time."

"Time for what?"

"Don't you think it's all been a little rushed?"

He looks a little put out. "Do you?" he replies a little harshly.

And I know I'm not explaining myself very well.

"I love being here with you, Edward, honestly I do, but don't you feel it's all been rather forced because of what's happened?"

"Is that how you see our relationship? Forced?"

"Now stop it – you're twisting my words. You know what I mean."

"I'm not sure I do. Because you told me you loved me, and if you love someone then don't you want to be with them? Isn't that the point of being in love?"

I roll my eyes. He's being defensive and I think I've hurt him.

"I'm not going to win, am I? Let's just forget I said anything," I mutter, and start to walk out of the kitchen.

"That's settled then – you're staying."

I huff, and head towards the stairs. He sounds so spoilt. I've a good mind to get a taxi, but I know that won't solve anything.

I sit on the bed, stewing, when there's a knock at the door. I look towards it as his hand pops through, waving. Then I hear a silly voice.

"Is it safe to come in?"

"Whatever," I say, but not aggressively.

"Is this our first fight?"

I huff again as he sits beside me on the bed, gently knocking my shoulder with his.

"I suppose I know what you mean, Abbie. You just throw me, that's all. I wasn't expecting you to say you wanted to leave."

"Edward, there's a difference between me going home, and leaving. And I've told you I'm not leaving just because you're a little kinky." His eyes raise. "I was saying it because …" I breathe out. "Because I just want that feeling – that feeling I've never experienced – of waiting in anticipation to get picked up. My heart racing as time ticks on. Long telephone conversations, neither of us wanting to put down the phone first. I've never had that before."

"And that's the only reason you want to go back home?"

"Yes, and it sounds silly now I've said it."

He smiles, then grins.

"What?" I ask.

"You, that's what. And the things you say. That's why it's so easy for me to love you."

"It is?"

"Yes, because you're so sweet, practically edible. Come on. I'll drive you round to your house if you like, although I'm not happy about you being there on your own."

I squeeze his hand because I know why.

"You stay until I've picked up my things if you like, and then drop me back home."

He grins. Home. His house.

It's snowing again and the air is bitterly cold as I sit and wait for Edward to finish scraping the windscreen. He wouldn't let me help saying there was no point in us both freezing our butts off. I just laughed and sat snuggly in the warm car.

He jumps back in. His teeth are nearly chattering.

"Bloody hell, it's freezing out there."

We drive to my house, discussing the party tonight. Well, I say discussing. It's mainly me doing all the talking and asking questions that I already know the answers to.

"I'm a little worried about tonight, but I am looking forward to it," I babble. "I'm quite excited, actually, and thank you for the dress. It's beautiful. Will it be really that formal?" He laughs, because he knows I'm nervous and he's already told me it's black tie.

"Maybe to start with, but I'm sure as the drink starts flowing, it'll get more relaxed. Are you really that nervous?"

I shrug.

"They're only people, Abbie. Alison and Tom are going."

I smile. "What if they start talking in medical jargon that I don't understand?"

He shakes his head and squeezes my knee. "If you feel uncomfortable, then we don't have to go."

"No, but I want to go, and I've not seen Alison for ages. This is what I wanted – us to go out together as couples and friends, enjoying ourselves. And I'm looking forward to it now," I say without taking a breath.

"Okay." He smiles. "If it gets a little too much, squeeze my hand and we'll move on."

"Deal," I say.

He pulls the Range Rover onto my drive. "I'll not be that long. Just bits for tonight and clothes for your parents' house."

"The hamper, Abbie – I never said thank you."

I smile. "It's a thank-you gift for inviting me. I didn't want to go empty-handed; that wouldn't have been polite. I didn't know what to get so Gran suggested the hamper. Do you think they'd like it?"

"They'll love it, and they'll love you, although you didn't have to do that."

"I know, but I wanted to. It's really nice of them to ask me."

"Oh … they're just being nosey. You do realise that, don't you? And you'll get the third degree from my mother and sisters – they'll want to know all about you."

"I think they'll find me rather boring, Edward – there's really nothing to tell."

"Nonsense," he says. "Come on. Let's get your stuff, and then back home so you can get ready while I call in at work."

We both get out of the car and walk up to the front door.

Chapter 14

I open the front door and stamp my feet to remove the snow from my boots, then walking into the hallway with Edward on my heels. The heat hits me, making my cold cheeks sting. The house is sweltering.

"Hell, Abbie, did you not turn the heating off before you left?"

"Yes, I set it to the winter setting so that the pipes wouldn't freeze," I answer, walking over to feel the radiator. "Ouch!" I yank my hand away, but not before feeling the burn.

"Let me see," he says. "Go and put it under the cold tap before it blisters."

I walk towards the kitchen, waving my throbbing hand.

"Where's the boiler, Abbie?"

"In the cellar." I point at the door next to the cloakroom. "The lights at the top and there's a pull-cord at the bottom," I shout. "And be careful of the steps; they're steep and worn in the middle."

It's dark with just the light coming in through the hallway, and the blinds are closed. I head for the sink, focusing on the cold tap. Gingerly, I turn it on and place my hand underneath. It smarts like hell. Then I wonder why the blinds are closed; I can't remember shutting them. I go to take my hand out of the water just long enough to open the blinds, but stop because I start to get a hot flush. The house is like a sauna.

Edward comes back up the steps.

"Abbie, the boiler was set on constant."

"No, it can't be. I remember setting it."

"Are you sure?"

"Yes, of course, I'm sure." I start to second guess myself, thinking about the blinds too, but think hard. "I remember doing it."

"Why are you standing in the dark?" he asks, switching on the light. I just raise my eyes towards him. "It must be faulty then."

"Let me see your hand." He takes it from under the water and I wince. "Is it hurting?"

"God, yeah, it's bloody killing."

"Stick it back under the water then. What do you need from your room?"

"I'll get them in a minute."

"Do you want the blinds open?"

"Yes, please. Just tilt them slightly."

My eyes follow him towards the conservatory and past the table, as I can now see the kitchen properly in the light.

I freeze. My heart skips a beat as I see a plate on the table, a glass, and a half bottle of whisky.

"Edward!" I shout, and he turns quickly.

"What's wrong?" he answers, walking hastily back towards me and removing my hand from under the water.

"It's not my hand," I say, staring in shock at the table. "They're not mine. I didn't leave them there before I left."

I feel flushed again as I realise what's going on; things are suddenly falling into place. The boiler, the blinds. And then I think about the cellar.

"Did you unbolt the cellar door at the top before you went down?" I blurt out.

He shakes his head, and an icy chill runs over my body.

"He's in the house," I screech.

"Who? Who's in the house, Abbie?"

"Adam! I put that bolt back on the door when I left, and I never closed the blinds. And those things on the table—"

"Are you sure?"

"Yes!" It's as if he doesn't believe me.

"Okay," he answers, holding his hand in the air. "Calm down, Abbie. Listen, there's no noise, no car on the drive." I nod. "You stay here and I'll check the house."

"No! Let me come with you."

"Abbie, he's not here. Put your hand back under the water and I'll check the house."

"Be quick, please," I say anxiously.

He nods and kisses me on the forehead head to reassure me. Then he leaves the kitchen.

I hear him running up the stairs, opening the bedroom doors then shutting them. He comes back down and checks the lounge, then the morning room and the old play room.

"He's not here, sweetheart, and he wasn't down in the cellar," he says, sounding a little breathless as he comes back into the kitchen.

"Are you sure you checked all the rooms? I mean in the cellar?"

"I'll do it now."

"I'm coming with you."

"I do think he's been back to the house though."

"That's what I've been trying to tell you."

"I know, but he's not here now … Maybe he just got his stuff and left."

I raise my eyes. "I hope you're right. I don't want a confrontation with him," I say bluntly, as we head towards the cellar.

I check the bolt. It's broken. The screws are hanging from the hinge and I know Adam's forced his way in through the cellar door.

"Look, Edward."

He nods but doesn't say anything.

I follow him cautiously down the cellar steps. Edward pulls the light cord at the bottom. I stop and notice a piece of wood over the window above the sink. The safety chain's not on the cellar door but dangling to the side. Leaves have blown in from outside and cover the floor near to the door. The gate bangs unfastened against the wall at the top of the steps. And I know I'm not imagining things because I distinctly remember locking that gate and checking the safety chain on the back door.

I following Edward into the cellar and walk over to the first room that leads off the main area. I need to know whether Adam's down here. I open it warily and stick my head inside. I breathe a sigh of relief when I see only the garden furniture. The other rooms are empty too. The door is open, and the padlock has been removed. At first, I'm a little apprehensive about looking inside, wondering why it was padlocked in the first place. I poke my head inside, unsure of what to expect. It's warm compared to the rest of the cellar. a radiator on the wall is throwing out heat. There's a television mounted on a swivel bracket above a desk, a DVD player underneath on a shelf, and a telephone socket with an internet connection. A large rug lies on the floor, and there are two filing cabinets with the drawers open, though the key is still in the lock. The drawers are empty. It looks like an office, one that's recently been emptied in a hurry.

I remember how when he worked at home he'd done it in the front room, usually sprawled on the sofa so that I could fetch and carry for him.

"An office?" Edward asks from behind me.

"He did all his work in the lounge upstairs."

"Well, it looks like an office to me."

"I never came down here, not unless it was absolutely necessary. It scared me too much. I got locked in once when I was a child – that's why my dad put the bolt on the door at the top of the stairs." He smiles at my explanation. "But one thing I did find odd before I went to the Lakes was the padlock on this door. I tried to shift it."

He listens as though he's picturing it in his mind, working something out. Then he steps back slightly and looks at the door, seeing where the padlock was mounted on to the frame.

"But as I was pulling at it, Marmalade, the cat from next door, spooked me by banging her paws on the window. So I left pretty sharpish. That's how I know I put the safety chain back on the door – I remember checking it to make sure it was secure. Then I ran up to the hallway and made sure I closed the bolt. I was relieved, knowing I'd not have to go down there again until I returned home. I remember doing all of that."

"I believe you. So that's how he got in – through the back door?"

"He left through the back door, yes, but came in through the window. See?" I point towards the splintered wood. "That wasn't broken either, and there were no leaves on the floor. He's forced the door at the top to gain access, and most likely he's taken a key."

"Come on. I think we should get your stuff and leave. Do you want to ring the police? Tell them he's been in the house? Well, broken in?"

"I don't think there's any point, do you? I mean there's not much I can do about it, is there? They've already told us that because it's still his home. Well, he thinks it is, though we know different. And he's only taken his stuff, I suppose, although I've not checked, and … oh, I don't know what to think anymore, and, frankly, I don't care either."

"You're being very calm about this."

"Is there any point anymore letting him stress me out? That's what he'll want. And I'm not biting, Edward. I've had an enough of him. And at the end of the day they're just things, and things can be replaced. Material thing matter to him, but they don't matter to me." I breath out long and hard. "But there is one thing I need to ask you, Edward." He nods. "Can I please stay with you?" He looks shocked, and I know it's because of how I'm reacting. "Can I please stay at your house? I don't want to come back here anymore, not now, not like this, always looking over my shoulder, wondering if he's been or is going to come."

"Of course you can," he answers immediately. "At least he's good for one thing, Abbie."

I frown, wondering what on earth he means.

"Like what?" I blurt out, stunned, but it doesn't faze him.

"It means I get to keep you now," he says. He walks over to me, kicking something on the floor as he goes. He glances down, then quickly back at me.

"What was that?" I ask.

He shrugs, placing an arm around my waist to move me forward.

"Come on. Let's get your things and leave," he says hastily.

And I know I can't wait to get out of here, and I just don't mean the cellar this time. I never thought in a million years I'd feel like this.

"Yes, let's do that."

He continues moving me towards the door, but then holds back a moment. I turn just as he's standing back up and putting something into his pocket.

"I dropped the car keys," he says as I stare.

We go upstairs to pack my things – just what I need for the party tonight and Edward's parents' house. I've not got the energy to even think about what Adam might have taken that wasn't his.

Edward puts my bags into the boot of the 4x4. I smile and wonder if he has any idea how much confidence he's given me – to do the things I've done and the things I'm about to do.

I realise it doesn't feel like my home anymore; it feels tarnished. Perhaps it hasn't been my home since my parents died. I thought the memories I had of them were grounded in this building, but they aren't. They're in my head, and I see that now. No matter where I am, I'll always have those memories, and I don't need this house to prove that to myself anymore.

I slam the door shut and turn the key. It's as though I'm locking my past inside. It's like I'm closing Pandora's box, putting all the sadness and pain of my past into storage.

"Are you okay, Abbie?"

"Yes," I say, taking a deep breath and putting the key into my pocket. "I'm going to sell the house … well, I'm going to tell Gran I want her to put it up for sale."

He looks surprised. "I thought you never wanted to sell it."

"Yes. I said that, didn't I? But it has too many bad memories, and they outweigh the good ones. I need to let it go. I don't want a constant reminder of the fact that for four years I lived here as a prisoner with a monster."

He holds his head to one side. I'm not sure whether he's just listening or shocked at my admission, but I carry on never the less.

"You've taught me to love, and to be loved. I lost my babies in that house. The memories of how I lost them are in that house, and they can stay in that house, because that's all it is. A house. It's not home and hasn't been for many years. The love I have for them is here." I place my hand over my heart. "They're imprinted here for ever, and nobody can take that away from me. My dreams of them have laid those demons to rest, and the final demon is gone." I smile warmly towards him and my voice lowers. "You've mended my broken heart, Edward. By loving me, but most of all by letting me love you."

"I have?"

I nod. His eyes close as he walks towards me with outstretched arms. And I walk into them.

"You're the most beautiful thing I've ever known. And I love you."

I smile, feeling safe in the strong arms that encase me. I'm not scared, or sad, or worried. He's taught me not to be. I just feel loved.

Chapter 15

We're still holding each other and I'm now so cold that my teeth are chattering.

"Let go of me and get in the car before we both freeze to death," he remarks.

I squeeze him one last time before releasing him, and he takes my hand. It makes me scream.

"What?" he shouts, looking around then back towards me.

My lip quivers. "My hand."

"Sorry!"

"Ouch!"

"Come on. I'll be quick in work. I'll dress your hand for you while we're there."

I nod, almost sulking because my hand is smarting so much. He runs a finger down over my nose and pouts. "Sorry," he says in a silly voice, and I manage a smile. "Now be brave, or no lollypop for you."

I giggle and get into the car, imagining Edward giving out lollypops to his patients. His eyebrows raise with a gleam in his eye, as though he's just thought of something.

"What?"

"Wait and see, Abbie."

"No, tell me. You're up to something, aren't you?"

He starts the engine. "Just wait and see."

And that's all he says as we drive towards the hospital.

We've arrive on the ward and go into the treatment room. Edward gestures towards the bed. A small gleam appears in his eyes, and he speaks in a smooth velvety voice, the one he tried his very best to woo me with right at the start and in this very same room.

"Take a seat while I get some dressings for your hand."

I sit on the side of the bed, swinging my legs and remembering our last time in here. Gosh he made my pulse race and my face blush. And that's not changed very much. I'd have put money on us never getting together, but look at us now. I thought he was arrogant, cocky, too damned good-looking for his own good. *Mmm, not much has changed there either*, I think. But would I change him? No, never. Gran's voice comes into my head. *Not for all the tea in china.*

"Why are you giggling, Abbie?"

I shrug. "Not for all the tea in china."

"Eh?"

"I was just remembering the first time we met in here."

"Mmm … we're a little different now though, don't you think?" I nod and smile. "Although what about the treatment room further up?"

I remember what I said outside the room, and how he overheard. Trust him to say something about that. I cough slightly.

"I don't know what you mean."

"Oh, but I think you do," he says, swaggering towards the bed.

I laugh, and that's what's so nice – that he makes me laugh.

"Oh, you find that funny."

I nod.

"Really?"

"Mmm …" I whisper as he parts my legs and walks into them. "Oh dear, I seem to have offended you in some way, Mr Scott."

"Would you like me to remind you what you said?"

I just smile. Then a silly noise leaves my throat as his hand runs up my back, drawing me in close to him. I can't deny it – those feelings are still there. I flush and my core tightens, and it's the same as always, tighter than the hangman's noose.

"I didn't mean it though."

"Oh, but I think you did. But I forgive you," he says confidently. Then he gets a dressing pack. "Hand," he says in a stern voice. I poke out my tongue. "I'll ignore that," he says as he looks at the burn. "Mmm … I think I might need you to lie down," he says gravely.

"Really?" I bat my lashes. "For my hand? Is it that serious?"

He nods, then grimaces, and takes a sharp intake of breath.

I try my best not to laugh.

"Might get a little tricky. You might even need to undress."

"Really? Whatever do you mean?" I reply flirtatiously.

"I wouldn't want you fainting on me again." He raises his brows dramatically. "Or having the fiasco we had last time. You remember – you nearly panting and drooling over me!"

"Me drooling over you? I seem to think it was the other way around."

"Me? Never? I never drool over women."

"Really? I bet I can make you drool right this very moment," I answer, licking my lips slowly.

"Nah … I'm sure you can't, but you can try if really want to."

"Oh, no … I'm not playing into your hands. I'm onto you, Edward Scott."

"Don't know what you mean. Now shut up and lie on the bed."

He leans forward and tries to push me down, grinning wickedly with that come-to-bed look in his eyes. My heart's racing at the hot look he's giving me, but I resist.

"Playing hard to get, Baxter?"

I laugh as he plants a sloppy kiss on my lips. We both jump as the door opens.

"Mr Scott, Abigail, sorry. I heard noises," Sister says. "I didn't know you were in here." She looks at me, then notices my hand "Oh, Abigail, what have you done to yourself now?"

"Hi, Amanda," Edward says politely, trying not to laugh.

Her eyes raise as if she's hearing him speak for the first time.

"Mr Scott, hmm … hi. Would you like me to take over?"

He looks at me and I shrug.

"Is that okay with you, Abbie? I'm sure Amanda is better at bandaging than me." We both look at him, shocked. "I'll go and make those phone calls. Will you meet me back in my office when you're done?"

I nod, taken aback by his admission that Sister is better than him at bandaging and him calling her by her first name.

"Well, nice to see you, Amanda."

He kisses me on the cheek, winks and starts towards the door. Then he turns. And it takes me back to the treatment room again and I'm wondering what on earth he's going to say.

"Give her a lollypop if she's a good girl."

Then he leaves and I'm almost certain he's laughing. Sister and I stare at each other, shocked by his behaviour, then we both laugh.

"Well, it seems you're the best thing that's ever happened to Mr Scott. In all the years I've worked with him he's never called me by my first name. He just gives out instructions and expects everyone to follow them, or they suffer the consequences."

I wonder how many times she's been on the receiving end of those consequences. I know I was at the beginning. Then I smile to myself, thinking, *Is Edward mellowing?*

"He's really very sweet," I add.

"Well, my dear, I think that's down to you, and you alone."

I smile again and go a little red, but think how nice it was of her to say so, and wonder if it's true.

"Anyway, let me see your hand. Oh, that looks nasty. What happened?"

I explain about the radiator and she shakes her head as she dresses it.

"You need to keep this dry and have it changed in two days. I'll pack some dressings for you," she adds as she's puts some into a bag for me to take home. "I'm sure Mr Scott will change them."

"So, I believe you're staying with Mr Scott."

I smile. News has got round fast. And I wonder if I'll be allowed back onto the ward where Edward is the consultant.

"Sister—"

"Please call me Amanda."

I nod. "Do you think they'll allow me back on this ward?"

"Of course …" She lifts her eyes. "Ah, I see what you mean, with Mr Scott. Best to ask them, dear. But I hope they do!" She leans forward, seeming to check that the doors are closed. "Can I be honest with you?" I nod, wondering what she's going to say. "I've never seen Mr Scott upset like he was when you were in ICU. It's obvious how much he cares for you. I shouldn't have said anything really, but I think you know that, anyway, don't you?"

"Yes, I think I'm coming to realise it." She smiles broadly. "You're really good for each other."

"May I ask you something?" She nods. "Can I have lollypop?"

We both laugh as she asks me which colour, and then, to my surprise, she pulls a jar of lollypops from the cupboard, takes off the lid and offers them to me.

"I thought he was joking."

"No. He buys them for the little ones. All of them are scared when they come in, but he has a wonderful way with children, putting them at ease straight away. They all leave with a bravery badge and a lollypop."

My heart suddenly melts, picturing him with children, making them feel safe just like he does with me. I reach down into the jar and take two. One for me and one for him, because I love him.

We chat a little more. I learn quite a bit about Amanda. She has six children, five grandchildren, and has been married since she was seventeen.

I leave the treatment room and head to Edward's office. I knock and wait for him to answer as I can hear him on his phone.

"Come in," he shouts. I enter just as he replaces the receiver. He looks up, winks and points to a chair.

I sit opposite him and look around his office, which I've not been in before. Umpteen certificates hang in frames from the walls. Awards for this, awards for that, countless academic certificates and hundreds of books on shelves. His desk is in the middle of the room. He sits on a swivel chair. Behind him is a window with a view of the hills and countryside. A computer, keyboard and a dictaphone sit on his desk, along with a picture that faces him so I can't see who's in it. He's notices me looking.

"Come here," he says, gesturing for me to walk round to his side of the desk. He passes the frame to me. It's of me. I'm in Alison's flat, curled up asleep in his arms, but I look like I'm smiling at him. I remember that day, though not him taking it of course. He watches my face as I smile and pass it back. "Do you know her?" He asks inquisitively.

"She looks familiar," I reply, rubbing my fingers under my chin, pretending to ponder on it.

"Gorgeous, isn't she?" he whispers.

I giggle. "Here, I've brought you something." I taking the wrapper of his lollypop and put it in his mouth. He looks a little stunned. "For being a good boy," I say, laughing then winking at him.

He pulls me onto his knee. I squeal as he removes his lollypop, putting it on to his desk, then kisses me hard and deep on the lips.

"Mmm … I'd love to take you over my desk."

"Edward Scott, you are the most insatiable man I've ever known."

He nods with that glint in his eye. "We could lock the door and close the blinds."

"That's not going to happen." He pouts. "Here," I say, as I put his lollypop back into his mouth. "Suck on that."

His hand runs up my back. "I can't help this impossible desire I have for you!"

"Hmm … flattery, as you know, Mr Scott, goes a long way, but not in your office, you naughty boy. And if you continue to be bad I'll take back the lollypop I've just given you."

"Well then, we better go and see if we can rekindle this friendship in my office at home. Would that be a little more to your liking, Miss Baxter?"

"Maybe, Mr Scott, if you're a good boy."

I get off his knee quickly before he changes his mind and decides to lock the door and close the blinds.

"Home then." He winks. There's hope and a promise in his eyes.

"Now tell me, please, Edward. Who's drooling?"

We're still laughing as we leave his office and make our way from the ward. Just as we're about thirty or so metres from the door, it opens, and guess who walks through with Emily? Oh, great. They see us immediately. Edward grabs my good hand. Darcy sees and I can almost smell the jealously. He nods at them both, and squeezes my hand gently. I know darn well what he's doing, but I don't stop him because deep down I love it. Emily stops and Darcy can't get past.

"Abigail, nice to see you're you better," Emily says genuinely, but I can almost read Darcy's thoughts. I don't, however, get to answer, as Edward does that for me.

"She's fine now, Emily. Now that she's staying with me."

I want to giggle because Darcy's face is almost green with envy. Edward knows exactly what he's doing as he releases my hand and puts his arm around me, hugging me in front of them both. It's almost like a warning to Darcy. My heart beats so hard I feel it thud. Then he kisses me on the cheek and Darcy's face has turned to red.

"That's nice," Emily says, but Darcy remains mute. Edward moves forward to indicate that the conversation is over. Emily takes the hint but Darcy remains still as we walk through the doors. As we enter the long corridor he turns to me and winks.

"You're bad, and very, very intimidating!"

His eyes raise. And I just want to kiss him.

We drive home and for some reason I can't stop grinning because the look on Darcy's face was priceless and I think he's a little pleased with himself. We reach the house and he pulls the beast to a stop. That's my new nickname for the Range Rover. Edward thinks it's rather amusing.

"Come on, get out."

"Okay. Why are you being so bossy?"

"Out of the car, I said, and inside. Quickly."

I frown, wondering if he's going to whip me straight into his office.

"Upstairs now."

"Eager, aren't we? I thought you wanted it over the desk in your office."

He shakes his head. "Upstairs and pack."

"What?"

"Upstairs and pack your things."

I frown again, wondering what the hell he means. But he starts laughing. "Go and pack your dress for tonight. I'll bring your bags up to you."

"What on earth are you talking about?"

"You'll see. Now off you trot."

"Edward—"

"Just do it, Abbie. I'll be up in a minute."

He goes to the car to retrieve my bags, leaving me with my mouth open, wondering what he's up to. Shadow follows me upstairs.

"He's strange at times, your owner."

Shadow wags his tail and follows me into the bedroom. I go to the dressing room and take my dress from the rail. It's a beautiful lush purple, very formal and very tight. I grin thinking it's going to take some time getting into it.

Shadow barks from the bedroom and I know Edward's come in.

"Are you ready, Abbie?" he shouts as I walk out with my dress. "Your bags are here." He points. "Get your things together. You have five minutes."

"Five minutes for what?" I ask puzzled.

"Before the taxi arrives to pick you up."

"What's going on?"

"You wanted that feeling, that excitement …" I nod. "Well, that's what I'm giving you."

I smile because I realise what he's done. I hold my hand to my heart, miming *Thank you*.

"You're very welcome."

And I could kick myself for ever doubting him.

I hear a horn pip as Edward strides towards the window.

"It's here."

He leaves the room with Shadow hot on his heels; they're like two peas in a pod.

I quickly finishing my packing, and I have to admit I've acquired the most ridiculous smile on my face.

I leave the bedroom with my dress draped over my arm and a small holdall with my other stuff in. Edward is in the hallway, talking to the taxi driver.

"Madam, please may I take those for you?"

I nod and he takes my things outside. Edward holds my hand.

"Come, Abbie, your car is waiting."

The driver's inside the car and Edward opens the door for me. "In you get. Seat belt on." He bends forward and I pull him close, kissing him hard and long, not wanting to stop.

He moves his lips from mine and I pout.

"The Noble, please," he says to the driver.

It's sounds grand and I feel like royalty as he closes the door and mimes, *You're drooling!*

I giggle to myself as the taxi pulls off. I'm heading for what I know is going to be the best night of my life.

Chapter 16

The taxi slows and turns into a sweeping, tree-lined drive. Sitting proudly at the top is the Noble. My eyes dart all over. I don't know what to look at first, and I imagine the gentry that must have visited in the past – women in ball gowns, men in breeches and waistcoats. I smile, thinking of The Manor House and my date with Edward.

The car stops at the entrance. I inhale a satisfying breath. Water cascades from two fountains into lily ponds that sit in front of a four-columned entrance porch. What a magnificent building. It appears to be Georgian in style, but of course I'm no expert on architecture; I just know what I like. And I like what I see. I wonder which Noble lived here back in the day. The driver gets out and goes to the back of the car.

I step out onto the gravel drive and head to retrieve my dress and bag from the boot.

"Miss, my instructions are to escort you and your belongings to reception."

I wonder what Edward's up to and follow the driver inside. It's bright with high-ceilings, and the smell of fresh pine instantly hits my nostrils. I turn and am greeted by the most spectacular twenty-foot-plus Christmas tree. It's decorated with large red and gold glass baubles that reflect the twinkling fairy lights chasing each other around the branches. Silver gift boxes secured with gold bows sit underneath. It reminds me of home. Home with my gran and grandad. And I suddenly feel warm inside.

A noise catches my attention. It's the familiar crackling sound of dry wood burning. I take in a gigantic fire surround with a lattice guard and move towards it. As I come closer, my shadow climbs the walls, jumping and twisting as if dancing in time with the roaring flames. It's hypnotising. I stare at the stone surround, following the carved coats-of-arms to the mantel twelve or so feet above. Two oversized silver candelabras stand at each end, each with numerous candles, and I wonder whether they employ very tall staff or the Noble once belonged to a giant. I walk past two oversized sofas either side of the fire. Plump cushions inlaid with animal tapestries are scattered about.

It looks so inviting, comfy, welcoming. I hover next to one of them and my shadow dances over it, as if beckoning me to sit down, relax and take the weight of world from my shoulders. Which is exactly the intention, I think.

I follow the driver to the reception desk. My shadow follows me, and it's as though I'm on a film set, one where I should whip out a wand and cast a spell or make a wish. And if I could, I'd wish for this day never to end.

My daydream is cut short by the smart, black-suited gentleman behind the reception desk. He asks my name, but before I can answer the driver speaks for me, leaving me with my mouth half open.

"Miss Baxter."

The driver announces politely, like I'm royalty. He places my bag on the floor but keeps my dress over his arm.

"Could Miss Baxter's bags and dress be taken to her room?"

The receptionist nods, then presses a button on the desk. It's all so formal, and I feel as though I should be wearing a dress with a bustle and behind me an entourage of servants carrying countless trunks and an array of ball gowns, but I play along, knowing Edward is doing this for me.

The driver turns and addresses me as if he's reading from a script – which he probably is, knowing Edward.

"Miss, have a wonderful time."

I reach for my purse. He holds up a finger to stop me, then nods, turns and leaves.

"Miss," says the receptionist, "you're in the Princes suite, just at the top of the staircase. I'll get the porter to bring your bags to your room." He passes me a key card and a little box. "Mr Scott asked me to give this to you on arrival." I smile, curious as to what's in the little white box. I shake it and something rattles inside.

He smiles and addresses someone behind me.

"Arthur, the Princess suite, please," he says to, I presume, the porter.

I smile as my dress and two bags are picked up by a spritely sixty-year-old, who heads off with them up the elegant stair case at about thirty miles an hour. I try to call him back because he's taken two bags, and I only had one with my dress, but it's too late – he's nearly at the top.

I reach the top of the staircase and look for my room. I notice the door is open. I go in and find the porter humming as he unpacks a bag. I see now that it's Edward's. He moves to unzip my bag. I nearly run over to him.

"Oh ... oh, thank you. I can manage that – it's fine ... honestly," I stutter nervously until he releases the zip. I breathe a sigh of relief because my bag holds host to some very special underwear that I'm planning to wear tonight, and it's most definitely only for Edward's eyes. He seems kind and nods politely, moving away from my bag, before making his way from the room. I'm now a little stumped, though. Am I meant to give him a tip? He seems to understand my confusion.

"It's all been taken care of, miss." And he leaves.

The box is still in my hand. My phone rings. I'm pleased when I see the caller info. Edward, 2.05 p.m.

"Hi. I'm here," I answer. "Wow, it's beautiful. The room is stunning. We're in the Princess suite." I pause for breath, but then continue like an excitable child telling a joke quickly to get to the punchline. "And we have a balcony that overlooks the grounds towards the river. Oh, did you send a bag in the taxi? The porter's just left, but not before he unpacked it for you."

He sighs. "Hell, Abbie, are you going to let me get a word in or are you going to babble all day?" He groans but there's a hint of laughter in his voice.

"Sorry. Sorry … it's … it's just that I'm so excited."

"Well, that's the whole idea," he says slowly.

"I know it is but, wow, you should see the bed. It's gigantic. It's a four-poster carved with animals," I say, unsure as I stare at them again. "I think they're animals and the posts are draped with white satin." I giggle as I run my hand down the cool fabric. And I can imagine him just rolling his eyes.

"I'll see the bed tonight," he says, even cooler than the drapes. "Now, have you got a little box?"

I nod, then remember he can't see me. "Yes."

"Then open it," he says, almost sounding exhausted.

"Just let me put you down on the bed."

I hear him titter as I let go of the phone and pick up the white box to open it. "What's this?" I ask with a giggle. I remove a small plastic bag and a roll of Sellotape.

"The bag is to wrap around your hand; the Sellotape is to secure it so it doesn't get wet when you shower or take a bath.

You need to be thinking of taking a bath around three, as Wendy from the Blue Spa is coming to do your hair and makeup at around four."

"Really?" I'm choked that he's arranged this for me.

"Yes, she is sweetheart."

"Thank you. God, you're fantastic."

He laughs. And, oh, I love his laugh.

"I wish you were here. I know I said I wanted the excitement, but I miss you already."

"You're bloody fickle, Miss Baxter. One minute you don't want me there, the next you do. I can't win," he mutters.

"Oh, you'd win every time, Edward, every time," I say, feeling all mushy inside.

"Goodbye for now," he says, but I know he's smiling really.

"Oh, do you have to go?"

"Bye, Abbie."

The phone goes dead. I pout. I'm getting good at pouting. I wander into the bathroom almost in a daydream, still with a stupid grin planted on my face. My eyes widen – it's the size of the bedroom I had at Alison's flat. It's elegant, with a white suite trimmed in oak and a large roll-top bath for two like the one we have at home. Thinking of home and Edward makes me sulk again, but then I grin wickedly, knowing there's always the morning. I look around the room and notice another white box on a little table next to the sink. There's a message printed on the top: "Open me."

So I do. Inside there's another note: "For you, Abigail x."

My favourite perfume, bath oil, body spray and moisturising lotion all in No. 5. I feel like crying it's so sweet. I turn towards the bath and start to run the hot tap. I pour a large amount of the oil into it. The heat from the water mixed with the oil fills the room with scent that instantly reminds me of my mum. A tear forms in my eye – not because I'm sad, but because I feel so happy and in love. My phone bleeps. A text. Edward, 2.55 p.m.

Enjoy your bath! Mmm ... I can smell you. x

I look around the room, wondering how he knew I was filling the bath. I suddenly think he's here, but I know he's not. I look at the text again. I got a kiss; he's never put a kiss before. I squeal with delight and ring his phone, but it goes to voicemail. His voice.

"Scott. Leave a message."

I hang up. Then my phone bleeps again. 2.59 p.m.

Only text. That's the new rule. x

I text him straight back. 3 p.m.

I love you! xxx

3.01 p.m. *Quite right too! Now get in your bath. Don't forget your bag. I wish I was there to massage oil into that delicate, soft, silky skin of yours. x*

A little daft noise leaves my throat as I tingle inside, wishing he was here with me as I text back. 3.04 p.m.

Me too! xx

I lie in the bath for ages, topping it up with hot water until I've made the skin on my good hand and my toes go all wrinkly. I breathe in deeply, smelling the perfume and remembering happy thoughts. I feel so loved and safe, as I stretch out, completely relaxed, and then remove the plug. The oil smells divine, and it's so silky on my skin. I wrap a fluffy dressing gown around myself and head into the bedroom. I'm enjoying myself, though I don't feel quite like I wanted to feel, not really. The waiting, the anticipation, the excitement? In reality, I feel a little lost, as though there's something missing. Edward should be here with me, and I know it's silly but he was right. *If you love someone then don't you want to be with them? Isn't that the point of being in love?"* And he's made his point, though in a very nice way, I must say. I sigh and text him. 3.45 p.m.

I don't want to be here on my own. It's not exciting without you. I want to talk to you face to face not on the phone or via a text. Yes, I'm fickle, but your point has been made. You were right – we belong together, and I'm sad without you here with me. xxx

3.55 p.m.

Tough!

I burst out laughing. The swine – he's making me stew. I poke my tongue out at the phone. There's a knock at the door, then a voice.

"Abbie, it's Wendy from the Blue Spa. May I come in?"

"Hi, Wendy. Yes, do," I say. I get up from the bed and let her in. "It's so nice to see you again. Are you okay?"

She smiles widely. "Yes, I'm fine, Abbie. And you?" She comes in pulling a small black case and places it on the bed. "Now is in here okay? What are we doing?"

I shrug.

"Well, Mr Scott said anything you want you can have."

I smile. "He did?"

She nods.

"Well just my hair and makeup, if that's okay."

"That's fine," she says, and looks around the room. "Oh, that dress is fabulous. Let's make you just as gorgeous, though that won't take me long at all."

I blush and laugh softly out of embarrassment.

"How are you having your hair today, up or down?"

"I'll leave it up to you."

We chat away about all sorts of things. Time seems to go quickly, and before I know it she's finished.

"Have a look in the mirror – see if you like it." She stands back, admiring her work.

I walk over to the mirror and stare at the person looking back at me. I barely recognise myself. My hair's in soft loose ringlets, and placed gently to the side. My makeup looks flawless, but most astounding is that my eyes look wide and bright, and I'm smiling. I look radiant – in love, happy and content with my life. Butterflies start to tingle in my tummy and I'm not at all sure why.

"Abbie, don't you like it?"

"I love it, Wendy. You're an absolute genius."

She laughs. "Well, it's easy working with you; you're a natural beauty."

I shake my head.

"It's about time you started to believe in yourself," she says firmly. "Now, do you need a hand getting into your dress?"

"No, thank you, Wendy, I'm fine. I'm sure I can manage to wriggle into it," I answer a little coyly, then lift my hand, showing her the bandage, but really not wanting her to see the sexy underwear I'll be wearing under the dress.

"Okay, if you're sure. I should leave anyway. I still have quite a few appointments."

I smile, thanking her once more before she leaves the room.

Now that I'm alone, I try to figure out how the hell I'm going to squeeze myself into my dress. I walk over to my bag and remove the delicate basque, the lace-topped stockings and matching thong. I giggle, thinking, *Who's going to be drooling now?* then wonder how I'm going to put them on.

My phone rings. I practically run over to the dressing table and swipe the screen. Alison, 6.15 p.m.

"Hi. How are you?" I'm so pleased to hear from her.

"We're here. What room are you in? I was so pleased when he said he'd changed his mind, and you were staying over. And he asked me to I ring you as you might need some help. Although he didn't say what with."

I smile, knowing he's thought of everything, though I'm a little baffled as to when he set all this up.

"I'm in the Princess suite. And I'm so pleased you're staying too!"

"The Princess suite? Get you," she replies with a giggle.

"I know. I feel like a princess today. I can't believe what Edward's done for me. Alison … can I ask you a favour?"

"Yes, off course. What is it?"

"Can you spare me ten minutes? I mean, can you come round when you're ready?"

"I'm ready now. What's wrong?"

"Nothing's wrong. I'll show you when you get here."

"Okay, give me five. I'll just tell Tom."

"Thanks. See you in five."

I place my phone on the dressing table, knowing I'll not feel so uncomfortable asking Alison to help me fasten the basque or my dress.

I remove my dressing gown and put on the lace thong and the stockings. The basque is next; it's boned, and fastens with hooks and eyes. I try placing it on backwards, and start fastening it, but I can't twizzle it round because of the bones and my bandaged hand. I remove the bandage and dressing; the skin's not blistered and doesn't hurt too much, but I still can't do up the bodice. I'll just have to suffer the embarrassment of Alison seeing me in this sexy little number. I blush as my phone bleeps.

Edward 6.35 p.m.

Piano bar, seven sharp! And don't keep me waiting! x

I laugh out loud, replying straight back.

Bossy, aren't we? xxx

I feel nervous, excited. I put my dressing gown back on and Alison knocks and comes in. We both squeal with delight and hug.

"Wow, you look absolutely stunning. Red really suits you."

She grins. "Well, I thought diamonds suited me better," she screeches, practically throwing her hand under my nose to reveal an engagement ring, and for some very silly reason tears well in my eyes.

"Oh my goodness! When?"

"This morning. I so wanted to ring you, but then I wanted to show you first. You're the first person I've told."

I throw my arms around her. "I'm so pleased for you. Tom's fantastic and will make a wonderful husband." My phone bleeps again, but I ignore it this time, too wrapped up in Alison's news. "Tell me everything."

She tells me how he proposed and it's so romantic that I hold my hand to my heart. That's when Alison notices the red mark from the burn.

"What have you done?"

I tell her everything and she's stunned.

"Well, you're far better off with Edward, and I'm sure nothing will come of it like you said. Like Edward said, bogus delusions."

I just nod, hoping she's right.

"So, I'm presuming you need help getting into that very tight dress."

My phone bleeps again.

"Sorry, I think I need to get this."

Edward, 7.10 p.m. I stare at the screen, hardly believing the time, then I grimace towards Alison, before reading the message.

You're keeping me waiting, Abbie. Do I really have to come to the room and get you?

There's no kiss this time and I think he's cross with me.

Sorry! I'll be five mins. Promise. xxx

But I get no reply, and in all honesty I wasn't expecting one, although he's made me feel jittery now, and I hate being late. But I've just been wrapped up with Alison's fantastic news and I've not seen her for weeks. She stares at me.

"Sorry. I was meant to be meeting Edward at seven in the piano bar downstairs, but it seems like I'm going to be late." I raise my eyes as she smirks. "And I need help with the basque too."

"Come on then. You get it on and I'll fasten it for you."

We're done. I'm in the basque and the dress, and gosh it's tight. It clings to my figure like a second skin and the basque underneath pulls in my small waist, making my figure appear like an hourglass. The split of the full-length dress starts at my left ankle and runs diagonally towards the top of my right thigh. I'm wary that it'll show the top of my stockings when I walk. My breasts at least are covered, with a small amount of cleavage showing, though if I breathe in too deeply or sneeze, I might pop out. But all in all, I feel very sexy as I put on my heels and brush my hand over the soft, cool satin.

"Hell, Abbie … you look like a model."

"Don't be daft," I say, walking over to the mirror to look. I stare at this woman looking back at me. I look like I belong on a red carpet. I can't believe it's me. My figure curves in all the right places; the split of the dress is sexy, but elegant. My hair shines brightly, and I've a grin as big as the Grand Canyon on my face. And it's all down to Edward. That amazing man who's given me so much confidence, a smile, and my life back. I blow out a deep breath.

"Well, I don't look that bad, I suppose."

Alison shakes her head at me, but I think she knows how I feel as she's been there for me from the day I met her.

"Get your bag and go and meet your date."

"Perfume first," I say. I spray it liberally, inhale the scent, then briefly close my eyes, alone with my thoughts. I grab my bag and follow Alison as she heads to her room to get Tom.

I feel nervous as I look over the banister. Edward's at the bottom of the staircase, pacing up and down and looking impatient. I hold on to the banister and make my way towards him, hoping I don't fall arse over tit. I giggle, thinking of the irony.

He looks at his watch. His foot's on stairs, as if he's thinking of coming up to get me. His hand reaches for the banister and his eyes look upwards. He nods when he sees me looking down at him. I notice his stare and my pulse races. I'm expecting a comment as to why I'm late and have kept him waiting, but he just breathes out, winks, and tilts his head to one side. That cheeky grin appears across his face as he looks at his watch again, and I mime, *Sorry*, knowing I'm at least half-hour late.

The tightness of the basque makes my bottom wiggle more than normal, and his eyes don't leave me; it's like he's devouring every step I take. And the expression on his face is hot, as if he's seducing me as I walk. I feel a blush creep onto my cheeks. My heart pounds in my chest, my palms feel clammy, and butterflies are doing every Latin dance imaginable in my tummy. So I concentrate on not falling. His eyes move down my body as I get closer, moving across the split in the dress then towards the top. They hold there for a second before turning to my face. A nervous noise leaves my throat as I can see what he's thinking; it's as though he's undressing me as I walk. I reach the bottom and he bends forward, holds out his hand, and blows out a very long breath.

"You look stunning. I forgive you for being late!"

I feel a little shy though I'm not sure why. "Thank you. You don't look so bad yourself."

A small smile flickers across his face.

"I can't believe that you're my date, Abbie."

I'm dumbstruck. Is he for real? He looks like he's just walked off the set of a Bond film, dressed immaculately in a black tux and with the sexy stubble on his chin that he knows sends me wild.

I breathe in deeply, and my breasts move upwards, revealing more of my cleavage. The smile that plays across his face tells me he's noticed. And I get an urge that I can't resist.

"Edward, I do believe you're drooling!"

He smiles and almost growls back his reply. "Miss Baxter … I do believe I am. Now, can I kiss you?" he asks, pressing his lips against my cheek.

His powerful arms move swiftly around my tiny waist. I giggle flirtatiously as I slide my hands into his jacket and feel the cool silky material of the shirt stretched over his muscular back. He pulls me closer and I run my nails gently down to his waist to hold him in place.

"I thought you'd never ask," I say, almost breathless.

Chapter 17

I'm in the ladies', brushing my dress down, smiling contentedly at the wonderful night I'm having, and listening to all the gossip coming from inside the cloakroom. Not that I'm being nosey; it's just taken me a little longer than normal, what with the dress and the basque. I've raised my eyes occasionally at what two women are saying. Maybe it's the drink talking, or maybe they think they're alone.

They're in front of my cubical, whispering loudly to each other, not realising I can hear every word that's being spoken.

"What's wrong with you? You've been jumpy all evening," says one.

"Can I tell you something in confidence, Claire?" says the other.

I feel a little intrusive, because I'm in here and they're out there, and she's going to tell her something in secret. I think I should leave and make it known to them that I'm here before she starts. But it's too late.

"It's him. He's here."

"Who's here, Betsy?" Claire says.

Betsy breathes out. "The guy I hooked up with at the last party you invited me to … he said I wasn't to say anything to anyone, but I wanted to ask your advice, because he's here and I don't want to face him. I've seen him but I don't think he's seen me."

"Did he do something nasty to you?"

"No, God, no … well, not really. I mean I was willing …" There's a silence again. It sounds as if she's struggling, and now I feel I really ought to leave, although I am a little intrigued about who this mystery man is, and what he's done.

"Remember the event at Easter when we went to The Drake."

My ears prick up at the mention of the Drake.

"Yes."

"Well that's where I slept with him."

"Really? That's not at all like you."

"Hmm …" She sounds more than disappointed with herself.

"And you're embarrassed because he's here?"

"No, Claire, not embarrassed. Well, sort of embarrassed … and, honestly, although it was months and months ago, I still can't get him out of my head, or what he did."

"What do you mean? You're talking in riddles. Just tell me what happened. I can't help you if you're not going to tell me what happened."

"Promise you won't tell anyone, please!" she pleads.

"I am your sister. Just tell me, Betsy," she replies firmly.

"Well, I told you I slept with him. Honestly, I've never had sex like it in my life. First it was hot and steamy, then it turned kinky. He did tell me from the start that he didn't make love, never has, that he just fucked and fucked hard, and that was a shock at first but a turn-on. But now I'm not sure whether it was a turn-on or down to the fact that he plied me with so much alcohol that I was unsure what I was doing. He continued asking if I wanted him to fuck me, which I did. But I'd have to do exactly what he wanted, with no questions asked, and foolishly I agreed. He tied my arms to the bedrail and my feet to the bottom of the bed."

A blush creeps onto my face, and my eyes are popping, but I'm also thinking, *Stupid girl – anything could've happened.*

"He did things to me, and I was turned on at first. I'd never orgasmed like that before in my life, and don't think I will ever again. I'd have done absolutely anything he asked at that point. And that's the problem – he knew I would."

I nod at that, because I've felt like that with Edward.

There's a silence, then Claire asks, "Did he hurt you?" The silence continues, and I want to ask her the same thing. "What is it, Betsy? Why have you stopped?"

"I'd rather not talk about the rest."

"Why? What happened?"

And that's exactly what I'm thinking.

"No, I don't want to say. But what I will say is when he'd done what he wanted to do and had satisfied himself, he left. I felt humiliated, angry, used and ashamed. I've not seen him since, until tonight, and I don't know what to do. I feel as if I should approach him and ask why he did what he did."

I nod. Claire blows out a large breath as I do the same, but my hand flies to my mouth so they won't hear me. I want to tell her to confront him — it sounds as if he's totally humiliated her.

"If you want to say something to him then do so. At least you'll know where you stand," Claire says.

And I think that's a little lame as she's meant to be her sister.

"You're right. I think I will," Betsy replies a little flatty, and I think I would too as it's not the response I'd want either. If it were my sister I'd be out there looking for him and giving him what for.

"What's his name?"

I wait with bated breath.

Betsy sighs. "You know him, I think."

"I do?"

"Hmm … he's a doctor at the Beaumont. Henry."

"Henry … I don't think I know a doctor called Henry."

"That's what he said."

They moving away from my cubical as a noisy group of women enter, talking loudly. I open the door quickly, wander out and mingle with the others. I look around, curious as hell to get a glimpse of this Betsy. I see two women, both slim, my height, one blonde and wearing a red cocktail dress, the other a brunette in purple. I wonder if they're Betsy and Claire, and Henry's identity is going to bug me all night. I make my way to the mirror, wipe my cheeks, which are still red from the X-rated story I've just heard.

"Abbie, God, there you are. What on earth have you been doing? The auction's about to start, and I do believe you've been entered."

"What?" I screech at Alison. "Who the hell's put me in the auction?" I shake my head. "Oh, let me see. Does his name begin with E by any chance?"

She shrugs and we walk out of the ladies' together.

"Come on. You've got to go to the stage."

"Really, I'm not at all impressed."

"Oh, but it's for charity. The children's hospice." I go with Alison to the stage, where a man with a clipboard asks my name. Alison goes to leave.

"You're not staying, or entering?"

"No, you have to be nominated by a man."

She leaves me listening to the rules.

"Each of you will be auctioned in turn to the highest bidder. When payment has been made, you sit alongside your bidder until the auction has finished. Then you have your first dance."

I suppose I can do that – one dance. Seeing as it's for the children.

"Then you belong to your bidder for the rest of the night." I glare at the man, thinking, *I don't think so. Belong to someone for money? Hell, what is this? A brothel?*

Edward stands at the bar. I can see him clearly from the stage. He glances around the room, then back at the stage as the man announces that the auction is ready to begin. I'm not at all impressed that he's entered me without even asking me. He notices me on the stage and his face suddenly changes; he looks annoyed. I huff, knowing he can't be as annoyed as I am, though I wonder why he looks so angry as it's obvious this was his idea.

I pull in a deep breath, and flash him a dirty look, just so he knows I'm livid. Then I make no further eye contact.

The auction begins, and I feel humiliated when the first two women are wolf-whistled off the stage by their bidders.

The man moves across to me, asking me questions I don't really want to answer, making comments about my figure and dress. It's embarrassing when the bids start. There's cheering and jeering as someone bids two hundred pounds. Edward turns sharply to see who's bid and I stare into the crowd, but it's dark and I can't make out who it is. His head turns back around towards the stage and he raises his hand to bid. I close my eyes as my cheeks flush, because all I want to do is walk off the stage, but I don't feel I can. I wonder why he's done this to me. Surely he knows I'd hate it, that it would make me feel self-conscious. All the while the auctioneer is making suggestive remarks as the bidding continues. I'm screaming inside as I see Edward's hand rise at eight hundred pounds, but it looks forced. I glare at him.

"Sold to the highest bidder. Now please come and collect your prize."

He makes his way to the steps. I move forward to walk off, but the man whispers, "Hey, be a good sport. It's for charity."

I wait for Edward to approach me. I'm furious with him.

"Here you go, mate. Your woman for the night."

He takes my hand and puts it in Edward's, then laughs at his own joke along with most of the room. Edward glares at me, then he squeezes my hand as I try to move it from his.

I'm breathing so hard that I nearly burst out of my dress. He sees and removes his jacket quickly, placing it over my shoulders to cover my nearly exposed breasts.

I knock it off and start ranting.

"How dare you do something like that to me."

He picks up his jacket and places it back on my shoulders, then moves me away from the stage to an area that's empty.

"Put it on. You're nearly falling out of that dress," he snaps.

I'm gobsmacked that he appears to be angry at his own doing.

"Well, was that not your bloody intention? You bought the dress for me to wear, and entered me into that cattle market. I didn't see Alison up there. Seems Tom has a little more respect for her than you have for me. Huh! Charity."

The words just keep flowing from my lips, like a fast-running stream. Words I'd never thought of before, let alone spoken out loud.

"What do I do now, sir? How much did you pay for me? Eight hundred pounds? Would you like a blow job under the table since I belong to you? Oh, I know. How about a quickie, here behind the curtains," I mock; And I know by the look in his eyes that I've hit the mark. I feel very hurt by the whole experience, and tainted by what's gone on, because this was meant to be my perfect evening. I pull his jacket off my shoulders. I feel insulted. "Here. Keep your lousy jacket. You've made me feel so cheap. And don't you dare follow me." My lip's quivering as I walk away.

"Don't you walk away from me, Abbie, and stop talking like that."

His voice is snappy. My eyes well. I can't believe he didn't expect me to react like this.

He grabs my arm.

"Let go of me, Edward."

I try to move my arm away.

His stare is harsh, and his eyes narrow as he holds his temper.

"Do you think I'd enter you into an auction for everyone to gawp at you? I know you wouldn't like it, and I certainly didn't like it. It wasn't me who entered you, and whoever said I did was lying. And for the record, Abbie, I'm just as fucking angry as you are – that you had to stand there while men bid on you when you're mine, and only mine."

I stare deep into his eyes, and I know he's telling the truth, though it doesn't change the way I feel about having to stand on that stage.

"Don't you believe me, Abbie?"

I nod. "Well then, if it wasn't you, who was it?"

He shrugs, picks his jacket up and holds it out to me. "Thank you. I need to fix my dress," I say, feeling powerless now. I should've known that he'd not do that to me.

His arm comes around my shoulder, squeezing it a little as if to say sorry, but he's nothing to be sorry for. I smile, wondering how many tiffs we're going to have before we finally know each other.

"I'll find out who did this, Abbie, and believe me, they'll be sorry for putting you through this ordeal."

"Oh, just leave it, Edward. It's done now. I know it wasn't you and that's all that matters to me. I'll be honest, I didn't like it, but what's done is done, and I suppose eight hundred pounds is going towards the children's charity." I sigh, just wanting to forget it now and get on with the rest of our night. We smile at each other.

"Do you want help with the top of your dress?"

I nod as he gently pulls it back up over my breasts.

"Do you want to stay?" I nod again. "Drink?"

"Yes, please. A double gin and tonic."

"A double?"

"Yes. I feel like getting drunk now, and I do believe you owe me a dance."

His laugh makes me smile. His lips go to my ear, nipping it.

"Mmm ... and I do believe you owe me—"

I slap his arm. He laughs, trying to make light of the situation, offering that olive branch that I'm getting better at taking. This is what he's good at, making me forget things that aren't relevant, and not dwelling on the past.

"A double gin and tonic and a dance – that's what you're getting, and be thankful for that!"

I giggle back now and his laugh is louder. His mouth opens, and I shake my head at him.

"No, Edward. I'd keep that thought to yourself ... at least for now."

As we walk towards the bar I hear a woman shouting at a man, and I recognise her voice. It's Betsy from the ladies'. I'm intrigued to see what she looks like. I turn towards the noise. Her back is to me. She's slim, with chestnut hair, and about my height, but I can't see who she's shouting at as he's standing behind a pillar. I'm hoping it's the guy she was talking about in the ladies'. My eyes widen as we walk near them. I feel as if I'm watching the last ten minutes of a drama before the big reveal, and desperate not to miss the end. So I hold back and make up an excuse to Edward that my shoe is rubbing my heel. I bend down, trying to get a better view.

"Why did you leave me tied to the bed," says Betsy.

Edward's eyes also raise.

"Are you all right, Abbie? Do you want a chair?"

I look up at him from the floor with a slight blush, thinking he's busted me for being nosey.

"No, no, it's fine … I just need to adjust the strap on my shoe. You get the drinks and I'll be along in a min."

He nods and walks to the bar. I continue to listen, pleased as punch that she's giving him what for. But then I see her hand go towards his arm, which is now in view.

"Don't you walk away from me. I'm not finished," she shouts. Then she suddenly falls backwards and a man looms over her face. I can't see him for the glare of the lights and the table that's blocking my view.

"Fuck off, you little slag."

I recognise that voice. I quickly get to my feet and make my way over to her. He scarpers quickly but not before I see his face. He glares at me with an icy look, because he knows I've just seen what he's done and said. And he certainly isn't called Henry. It's James. I knew from the start that there was something dodgy about him. And as for what he did to Betsy. I was right all along – he's just like Adam.

I reach her and offer my hand.

"Oh, God, are you all right?"

She looks stunned. "Let me help you up."

"But he can't get away with that."

"Trust me. Let him leave. Have nothing more to do with him."

She stares at me, puzzled, I think, as to why I'm giving her this advice. I roll my eyes. I don't think I need to say anymore.

Edward walks towards me with two drinks, looking confused as to why I'm now standing with my arm around a woman. I shake my head discreetly. *Don't ask.* His eyes raise in understanding.

"Would you like to come to our table for a few moments and wait for your sister?" Then I clam up, knowing I shouldn't have said that. But she nods and we make our way to the table and sit down. I offer her my drink. Edward's still looking puzzled. I mime, *I'll explain later.*

"Thank you for that," she says.

"I'm Abigail."

"Betsy," she says, holding out her hand.

Alison and Tom arrive back. Betsy looks embarrassed as they sit down.

"Alison this is Betsy. She tripped in her heels and she's just resting her ankle for a minute."

Betsy smiles and Alison says, "Do you work at the hospital?"

"No. I've come with my sister. She's a doctor at the Beaumont."

"Oh, what's her name? Tom or Edward might know her."

"Claire. Claire Davenport. Do you know her?"

"No, I don't think so. Edward do you know her?" asks Tom.

Edward shakes his head before taking a large drink. Then he pats my shoulder and mimes, *Going to the loo*. I smile and nod, knowing this night is turning out very different than I'd imagined and I'm also wondering what he must be thinking.

"Oh … here's Claire now," Betsy says, waving in her direction over my shoulder.

I turn and see a blonde-haired woman in a red cocktail dress about three or so tables away. She nods at Betsy, but stops in front of Edward, who's trying to make his way past her. She starts talking to him, but he pushes away a chair that's blocking his way. Her hand moves towards him to stop him and he seems uncomfortable. She speaks and he shakes his head. She reaches into her bag, removes a card and places it into his top pocket. Then she moves close to him but he moves back again. She reaches out her arm and he shakes his head again, taking the card from his pocket and putting it back in her hand. She grabs his hand and pulls herself towards him.

I sit, wondering what the hell she's playing at. Who is she to Edward? She grabs his waist, and kisses him on the mouth. I fly from my chair and march over to them. Edward looks uncomfortable. I take her arm from Edward and she stares at me.

"Oh, is this your date, Edward? But didn't you buy her in the auction?"

He looks at her, then at me. First I'm taken aback, then furious.

"Excuse me?"

She winks with a half-smile. "He paid more for me at Easter. I'd watch him – he's a slippery fish. Uses women."

"And how on earth do you know that? And more to the point, how do you know I'm not using him?"

Edward looks stunned but I'm not in the mood for a confrontation over one of his one-night stands, because it's evident from the remark she's just made that this is clearly what she is.

She just laughs as if to say *I warned you*, before turning her back on me.

I'm sick to death of woman like her, and men like Adam and James.

"Hey, I've not finished."

Her head spins round, whipping her long blonde hair around her pretty little face.

"He's got a girlfriend, and I suggest you go and find your own date, while you still can."

And, clearly, she's taken my warning on board, as she looks at me, doesn't answer whips her head around again and walks off.

"Hell, Abbie—"

"Any more of them here tonight, Edward?"

"I didn't take her up on her offer," he says, a little defensive.

"I saw everything."

"Then you know I didn't. I told her I had a girlfriend and that you lived with me."

"You did?"

"Yes, I did. What did you think I was going to do? Hook up with her? Don't you trust me?"

"Did you sleep with her?"

"I'm not getting into this conversation with you, Abbie. I also have a past, one that I've not hidden from you either."

I nod. It's true but I was jealous as hell when she kissed him.

"This night is not going as I'd imagined." I sigh.

He smiles. "Then let's get it back on track."

"And how do you propose we do that after all that's happened? Betsy, the auction, and her."

"You were jealous?"

I nod.

"Me too!" he answers.

I raise my eyes at his honesty.

"You do know I'd have paid any amount of money for you in that auction just to stop another man dancing with you!"

"Yes, I do."

He smiles then holds out his hand as a catchy number starts playing. I take it, and he spins me into his arms and holds me there. I squeeze him tightly, and he taps my bottom and growls.

"Now get your arse on that dance floor, you owe me a dance…or I'll drag you to our room and peel you out of that dress."

My heart pounds and my chest moves quickly. He watches my face with a dark smile, then his eyes run down the full length of my body and back to my face. I imagine him peeling me out of my dress. And he has the same thought – his eyes tell me so. But they're also telling me he doesn't want to make love to me; he wants to have me, and I want him to. I nod my head, letting him know what's on my mind. His eyes raise and he breathes deep as he takes my hand and practically drags me towards the stairs and up to our room.

The door slams, making me jump. Edward removes his jacket, then dicky bow, and throws them onto the floor. Somehow he doesn't need to speak; I know what he wants. I turn my back to him, and he walks into me, pinning me to him, pressing hard until I feel his erection. His hand runs from my neck, over my breast, and down to the split in my dress. His hand slides through and he tugs at my thong then slides it over my thighs.

All of my senses are on alert. Every nerve burns with desire. I moan as his hand goes to the zip of my dress pulling it down quickly, nearly ripping the dress from my body as he said he would, leaving me standing in my basque and stockings.

I step out of the dress and bend slightly to remove my shoes. His hand goes into my hair, pushing me further over so my head's on my knees. He moans, pulling my hips until my bottom touches him. He thrusts hard, making me jolt forward. His hand slips to the front of my neck and his fingers span my throat as he pulls me back upright against him. He breathes heavily into my ear as his hands glide over my breasts, lifting them from the basque and exposing them.

"Turn around," he commands. His tone of voice makes me do it, and though I'm uncertain I am willing.

I turn slowly to face him. His eyes close briefly, and when he opens them I see a look that's nothing short of predatory. He takes my breasts in his hands then moves his mouth onto them, suckling and nipping. I feel the sting in my nipples, and the sensation forces my head back and my eyes to close.

He tugs my hair, bringing my head forward, and takes my mouth hungrily.

I move close into him. One of his hands darts between my legs, and he cups my sex firmly, applying pressure. With the other he pins my hands behind my back. My heart nearly leaps from my chest as my body tingles with an intensity that makes my legs go weak.

His voice is low and fleshy. "You want me touch you, Abbie? Put my mouth on you?"

I nod desperately.

"Then ask me. But you will do it my way."

I swallow, unsure what he means by *my way*, but I don't care because I'm so aroused.

He takes one of my hands and places it onto him, holding it there for me to feel, and I pant heavily.

"You want this inside you?" His bluntness turns me to jelly and I can feel the heat on my crimson face.

I nod.

"Then sit on the bed."

His voice, his look, makes me do it. I turn slowly, not trusting my own legs to keep me upright. I sit facing him. A rough noise leaves his throat.

"Open your legs and let me look at you."

I opening them slightly.

"Wider, Abbie."

I'm shaking with so much adrenaline and excitement that I'm sure he can see it radiating from me. His chest moves rapidly, and his erection is nearly bursting from his trousers.

"Good girl. Now place your hands on your legs near your knees and push them open wider."

My hands tremble. He stares at my sex and waits for me to do as I'm told.

"Push them open, Abbie."

I place my hands slowly onto my splayed legs and push them open wider. And his eyes, they're in control, pleased that I'm doing as he says.

"Now run your left hand up your thigh and back down to your knee."

I stare at him.

"Do it."

I run it up my thigh, over the lace-topped stocking and the ribbons that are holding them in place. I close my eyes, feeling a little embarrassed. I know I'm blushing but my heart's also racing in response to his domination.

"Open your eyes and look at me." I do as he says, but his eyes are following my hand. "Stop!" he shouts, making me jump. "Run your hand inside your thigh slowly." And I comply. "Now touch yourself, Abbie."

My eyes fly to his and I shake my head. I can't do that.

"Do it."

"Edward, I can't."

But the hunger in his eyes demands it.

"I want to watch you touch yourself, Abbie."

I'm still shaking my head, but I want to please him.

"Please, Edward, don't. Don't ask me to do that. I can't."

He takes my hand and pulls me up.

"Will you let me help you then?"

I'm puzzled as he moves me towards the mirror. He turns me so my back is to his chest. One hand runs down the inside of my thigh, and spreads my legs. I stare at him in the mirror as he watches my blushing face. He takes my hand and places it between my legs.

I quickly try to move it, but he whispers, "Just try, Abbie."

His hand goes over the top off mine, guiding it and applying pressure. A gasp leaves his throat, as his hand moves quicker over mine, forcing mine to move. A pulse hits my core as I watch his face in the mirror. My cheeks redden again, knowing he's going to make me orgasm.

His hand leaves mine and I freeze as it goes to my breast. He puts his mouth on the side of my neck.

"Let go, Abbie. Don't be shy. Do this for me."

His eyes beg me; his voice pleads. And, slowly, I move my hand over myself, feeling the tingle and the rush. It's intoxicating watching him in the mirror, wanting me to continue. My core is tightening and my legs tremble.

"God, Edward, I'm coming."

I'm shocked as he places his hands under my arms, almost throwing me onto the bed, splaying my legs open. I gasp as his head dips between them, and I continue to climax as he greedily devours me.

I beg him to stop, ripping at the sheets. My body is sensitive to every touch and I can't stop shaking. I move my hand, trying to push his head away, but this only adds to his eagerness as he holds me firm. I climax with such force that I grab at his hair and nearly suffocate him as my legs clamp tightly. I can't catch my breath and pant heavily.

But it's not over. He pulls my legs apart then pins my hands above my head with one hand.

"Hold still. I'm not done with you yet."

His eyes are glazed as if in an erotic trance, and I whimper as he takes me again.

He releases my hands, stands quickly and almost rips off his trousers, followed by the rest of his clothes. His expression is sultry and I know it's not over. He strips me naked.

"Now I'm going to make love to you."

He moves inside me slowly. My eyes close.

"Open your eyes, Abbie, and look at me."

I open them and he thrusts deep. I feel every nerve tingle in my body as he repeats the movement. My legs begin to stiffen, but he holds back, waiting for them to relax. He repeats the motion until I nearly orgasm, then stops again, watching my face.

My eyes roll as the tingle slows. He's immersed in the control he has over my body. He kisses my breasts. My hands find his hair; my mouth reaches for his, but his is ravenous, greedy. He pulls out of me. My eyes move to his and he stares at me. I don't know what he's thinking; all I can see is hunger. He holds himself and I swallow as he sinks into me again, slowly thrusting and rolling his hips. I run my hands over his wet skin and my lips over his face.

He slows, holding back again, and I beg with him to continue.

His eyes are full of lust, and he ignores my pleading.

"I want to watch you crumble beneath me."

He pushes deep and hits my sweet spot. The sensation is strong, stronger than ever before, so that I nearly stop breathing. He knows it, and repeats the movement, watching me powerless beneath him. An almighty wave crashes over me. I scream in pure ecstasy. But he stills again. My eyes close, wondering why. Is this *his way*?

I open my eyes to meet his gaze, and his appear to be reaching straight into my soul, hypnotising me, and I realise that this is what he wants – for me to give myself fully to him. Committed, trusting. I breathe in deeply, understanding, nodding my head. His eyes haven't left mine, and now I see passion and craving. They're luring me into his web – one that I've held back from for so long, too scared to go into because I was so uncertain of what it held for me.

But it held him. Waiting for me. Waiting for me to trust him and love him. And I see that now.

"Yes," I whisper. "Yes, Edward. I love you with all my heart. I'm yours."

He doesn't speak but moves to my mouth and kisses me slowly. Then he moves inside me, and I feel the world move with us. Because this feels so different, and as he gently slides deeper inside I feel every inch of his love, his passion, and I feel close to tears as I crumble willingly. I feel him completely consume me as our bodies move together as one, and it brings me to tears.

. We're both breathless, He's collapses on top of me covered in sweat, and my head is somewhere, but not on my shoulders at this moment.

"Edward, you're going to have to move. I can't breathe."

He rolls to the side and pulls me quickly onto his chest.

"God, I love you, Abigail Baxter."

And I'm unable to speak. I almost have to fight for air, afraid of crying again, because I know he's my world, and that I'd do anything to keep it that way.

We lie in each other's arms, kissing and smiling until our breathing returns to normal, and my head returns from the clouds and plants itself back firmly onto my shoulders.

"I love you too, Edward Scott," I whisper.

He winks and moves up towards the top of the bed, patting it at the side, and holding the duvet back.

"Are you getting in?" he asks.

I nod, lie by his side and place my arms around his chest and my head on his heart.

"Mmm … this is where I like you – on my chest and falling asleep."

I smile and close my eyes as fatigue hits. I feel the duvet being placed over me. A kiss to my head. His strong arms holding me. And I feel lighter than the feathers that cover me.

And I know that Christmas with Edward is going to be the best in the world. And I can't wait.

Mended

Mending is only the beginning

By Adele Lea

Book 4 of the Abigail's fate series.

Out soon and available from Amazon book store.

www.Amazonbookstore.co.uk. Paperback.

www.amazonkindle.co.uk. Kindle edition.

Made in the USA
Middletown, DE
29 April 2018